Daria dive[...]
his chest.

His thick arms swung her around and they fell into the back seat, protecting the little girl inside. Bullets thudded into the surrounding vehicles. Daria shot a quick glance at Emma and shimmied out of the car with her pistol in hand.

She radioed for backup. "Shots fired! I repeat. Shots fired." She located the black Suburban in the distance as it disappeared down the street. "Black Suburban. No plates."

"Emma!" Jake pulled the screaming baby from her car seat and stepped out of the car. He held her firm against his chest.

"She looks okay. The blast of the gun must have scared her."

Emma reached for Daria. Surprised, Daria holstered her weapon, took the baby and wrapped her arms around the trembling bundle. Her heart squeezed. It had been a while since she'd held a baby, and it felt good. Jake tucked a pink fuzzy blanket around Emma and her cries grew silent.

Daria didn't need any more convincing. Someone was out to get Jake.

Or was it Emma they wanted?

Loretta Eidson is an award-winning author born and raised in the South. She lives in North Mississippi and enjoys family time with her four children and thirteen grandchildren. Her love of reading began at a young age when she discovered Phyllis A. Whitney's mystery novels. Loretta believes in the power of prayer and loves putting her characters in situations where they must trust God to pull them through tough situations. Visit Loretta on her website at lorettaeidson.com.

Books by Loretta Eidson

Love Inspired Mountain Rescue

Pursued in the Wilderness
Blue Ridge Mountain Escape

THE MARINE'S DEADLY REUNION

LORETTA EIDSON

LOVE INSPIRED
INSPIRATIONAL ROMANCE

LOVE INSPIRED®
INSPIRATIONAL ROMANCE

ISBN-13: 978-1-335-46849-9

The Marine's Deadly Reunion

Copyright © 2023 by Loretta Eidson

For questions and comments about the quality of this book, please contact us at CustomerService@Harlequin.com.

Love Inspired
22 Adelaide St. West, 41st Floor
Toronto, Ontario M5H 4E3, Canada
www.LoveInspired.com

Printed in U.S.A.

He that dwelleth in the secret place of the most High shall abide under the shadow of the Almighty. I will say of the Lord, He is my refuge and my fortress: my God; in him will I trust.
—*Psalm* 91:1–2

To my husband, who loved, supported and cheered me on during his last days.

Kenneth, I'll love you forever. Rest in peace.

Thank you, God, for Your mercy and grace.

ONE

Sergeant Daria Gordon cruised her hometown of Kimbleton, Missouri, one last time before she headed back to the police station to clock out. With temperatures dropping into the teens and the threat of a wintry mix, she could hardly wait to curl up by the fireplace in her new festive red pajamas. Just the thought of watching a Christmas movie and eating hot buttered popcorn made her mouth water.

The afternoon tourist traffic bottlenecked at the fork in the road in front of the Marketplace Grocery, which was nothing unusual for the Christmas season. A disturbance in the store's parking lot caught her attention. Two men scuffled between parked cars.

"Checking a fight between two male suspects in the Marketplace parking lot," Daria reported on the radio clipped to her uniform. She flipped on her flashing lights and siren, made a quick turn and pulled in behind a white SUV. Parking lots were private property, but she'd cruise by anyway to make sure no one got hurt.

A bearded man bolted and hopped into the passenger side of a waiting black Suburban. Tires squealed on the asphalt as they sped away. His opponent held a

pistol, turned and stuck his head into the back seat of
the white SUV. The one with the weapon was Daria's
top priority. She must secure the threat.

She opened the door with her weapon drawn and
eased from her squad car. "Police. Put your gun on the
ground and place your hands on your head where I can
see them." She readied herself for an abrupt reaction.

The suspect placed his pistol on the pavement and
pushed it toward her with his foot. He lifted his hands
in the air and stepped away from the SUV's back door,
sporting a busted lip. The sleeves of his camouflage T-
shirt bulged over his muscular biceps. She maintained a
watchful eye and studied him. He looked familiar. That
squared chin and those deep brown eyes reminded her
of someone she used to know.

"I'm not the one you want." His warm breath fogged
in the freezing temperatures. He glanced inside the vehicle and back at her. "You should've gone after those
guys."

"I'll make that determination. You're the one I saw
with a gun. Don't make any sudden moves." She adjusted her stance. "Back up." She eased forward and secured his weapon.

"That guy tried to take my baby. I had to protect her."
He let out a huff. "I'm Jake Fisher. Want my ID?"

"Yes. Take it slow. Why would someone want to take
your baby?" A slight lean, to glance inside the vehicle,
confirmed a baby was inside. A little girl about eighteen months old stared at her with tear-streaked cheeks
and a red nose that proved she'd been crying. The icy
December wind didn't help matters. "Hello, little one."
Daria smiled.

Poor baby. She must be freezing.

The child's eyebrows lowered. "No." Her lips pooched out.

She clutched a small rubber bunny in one hand and slapped the air toward Daria. Most children didn't like strangers getting too close, and her apprehension of Daria was a natural response.

"It was probably someone who works for whoever forced my sister's car off the road and killed her and my brother-in-law. You should go after them right now."

Daria reported the parking lot incident on the radio clipped to her shoulder. She gave a description of the black Suburban that had sped away. No license plate. Maybe the store's security camera captured the incident. She holstered her weapon as Jake handed over his driver's license, showing an out-of-town address.

"What's the nature of your visit to the Ozarks? Kimbleton, Missouri, is a long way from California." *Jake Fisher?* Could he be her scrawny best friend from middle school? If so, he'd grown some muscles. How many times had they talked about what they wanted to be when they grew up? He'd dreamed of becoming a professional football quarterback, and she'd thought about nursing. From the looks of his military attire, he'd changed his mind, as had she.

"I just returned from active duty after receiving word of my sister's death. She left me everything she owned." He pointed to the SUV. "She lived in the Ozark Mountains valley along the county line."

"Who was your sister?" Daria's curiosity stirred. Would he give the name she remembered?

"Amanda. Our family used to live here, but Dad

moved us when he received a job transfer to California." He shuffled his feet and looked around before returning his attention to her.

It was him. The first guy she'd ever had a crush on. He'd matured well and was more handsome than ever. She'd gone out with several of the local guys through the years, but they weren't to her liking. Dating was the last thing on her agenda right now, although seeing Jake again might move it up the list. She couldn't give in to her attraction. He had a baby, which meant he was already taken.

"I remember Mandy. Jake, I'm Daria, in case you didn't recognize me." Her heart thundered.

"I thought you looked familiar." He rested his arm on the open car door. "Thought you wanted to be a nurse."

"Well, I thought you were going to play football."

With a mature and brawny Jake standing in front of her, memories of all the fun they'd had as kids resurfaced. Was he still the easygoing guy she remembered?

Didn't matter. She had to focus on proving herself an efficient, well-trained cop. Especially after her supervisor's warning to get control of her anger issues. That disruptive vacationer and his dad six months ago had gotten on her last nerve. Richard and Tony Schneider. She'd never forget their names. She'd scolded the belligerent son in front of a crowd. He became hostile, so she arrested him. His dad wasn't much better, but she'd let his angry remarks slide. She'd worked hard to get this job and didn't intend on losing it or being assigned to desk duty.

The child's cry drew her back to the present. What was she thinking?

Stay focused on the incident.

Daria relayed Jake's personal information to dispatch. "Officers are on the lookout for the vehicle," she told Jake, then waited while the department looked him up. Once they confirmed Jake had an unblemished record, she handed his pistol back to him.

She'd been so focused on Jake that she hadn't noticed Christmas music playing through the speakers of the shopping center across the street.

A gust of wind cut through her clothes and sent chills to her toes. She zipped up her police-issued jacket. The child had to be freezing, too. With sleet and snow in the forecast, the roads were sure to be treacherous after nightfall. How could he stand there in the cold wearing that short-sleeved T-shirt? And where was the baby's mother?

"You might want to turn some heat on in your car. I'm sure your little girl is cold." Daria observed his gentleness toward the child as he tightened a pink blanket around her legs, then started the vehicle, adjusted the temperature setting and turned the fan on high.

"Should've thought of that myself. Thanks." He straightened and faced Daria, holding the door ajar. "No disrespect, but if you'd left me alone, I could've caught up with that car and taken care of the situation." His lips tightened. "I was a sergeant in the Marine Corps, so I've had plenty of experience with enemy tactics."

A woman wearing her heavy coat and carrying a bag of groceries hurried by them toward her car. She stared at them in passing. Daria nodded at her. "Hello, Caroline. I hope you and Mr. Hall are doing well."

The lady wasn't the social type and didn't respond,

but since she was the bank president's wife, Daria wanted to acknowledge her presence. Caroline slid into her car and drove away.

Daria looked back at Jake.

"Excuse me? I'm glad you're back in Kimbleton, and I appreciate your service to our country, but you're not in Afghanistan anymore. I'm the authority in this town, and this is my jurisdiction. You cannot take the law into your own hands, regardless of your experience." She stared into his determined eyes and bit back the agitation rising inside her. "Besides, if you had chased after them with this child in the car, I could charge you with endangerment to a minor."

"Didn't mean it like that, and you're right. I've got to protect Emma." His fingers swiped over his military haircut. "Someone is following us, and I wondered if he was the same person who murdered my sister and ransacked her house."

"Murdered? I heard of an Amanda killed in an accident, but the last name wasn't familiar. I never associated her with your family until now. I'm sorry for your loss, but there's been no report of foul play."

"Police report said they lost control of their pickup and crashed. They claimed it was an accident, but Amanda had been saying someone was after her. She was a cautious driver. I know my sister, and that wreck was not an accident." He rubbed his arms and pulled a jacket out of the car. "It was murder."

"You can't go claiming murder unless you have proof." He sounded so certain. The Jake she remembered never exaggerated; well, maybe when they were kids and he pretended to be a quarterback.

"I intend to prove someone killed her." Jake's jaw tightened.

She'd have to do some digging on her own to verify his story. "I'll see what I can find out. In the meantime—"

Tires squealed. The Suburban was back, and it raced up the parking lot an aisle over from where they stood. The passenger window rolled down and the barrel of a shotgun stuck out.

Daria dived for Jake and slammed into his chest, which was like hitting a brick wall. His thick arms swung her around and they fell into the back seat, protecting Emma. Bullets thudded into the surrounding vehicles. Daria shot a quick glance at Emma and shimmied out of the car with her pistol in hand. How the two of them fell in through that door at the same time, she didn't know.

She radioed for backup. "Shots fired. I repeat. Shots fired." She located the black Suburban in the distance as it exited the large parking lot and disappeared down the street. "Black Suburban. No plates."

Daria backed up closer to Jake. As an authority figure, she'd tried to protect both of them, but his strength had overpowered hers, landing them in the car. Should she be mad at Jake or thankful?

"Emma." Jake pulled the screaming baby from her car seat and stepped out of the car. He held her firm against his chest. Her shrill cry made Daria want to hold and comfort her. He dangled Emma out in front of him. Daria checked her body and clothes for blood. "Are you hurt, baby?"

"Ma-ma." Her fingers went to her mouth. Jake wrapped his arms around her again.

"She looks okay. The blast of the gun must have scared her." Daria scanned the area for the car's return. Sirens sounded. Help was on the way.

Emma reached for Daria. Surprised at the child's interest in her after her earlier response, Daria holstered her weapon, took the baby and wrapped her arms around the trembling bundle. Her heart squeezed. It had been a while since she'd held a baby, and it felt good.

Jake tucked a pink fuzzy blanket around his baby's body. She laid her head on Daria's shoulder. Her cries grew silent. Daria didn't need any more convincing. Someone was out to get Jake.

Or was it Emma they wanted?

Jake stood close to Emma while Daria held her. "Am I free to go? I've got to get her out of the elements and out of danger. They could come back with more weapons."

He could still hear the fear in his sister's voice over the phone as she begged him to take good care of her baby mere days before her death. She said if anything happened, he had sole custody of Emma, his niece. Two weeks later, they summoned him home. Police located his brother-in-law's pickup bottom side up off the mountain road. Both were deceased at the scene.

Whoever killed them would pay. Seeing death in a war zone was one thing, but losing family cut deep, and it put him on edge and on high alert.

He chewed his lip as uncertainty boiled inside him. Wars he could handle—shooting guns, maneuvering stealthily and securing the enemy—but he knew nothing about taking care of a baby. His aging parents weren't physically able to care for her on a day-to-day basis. Even though he was thankful Emma was with them when his sister's accident happened.

Asking for help from his ex-fiancée wasn't an option. The Dear John letter she'd sent him while he was deployed said it all loud and clear. How could she ditch him like that? He was on his own.

"Jake, are you listening?" Daria's hand squeezed his forearm. His muscle tensed. "I said you're free to go, but I'll escort you and Emma home." She handed the child back to him and walked toward her car.

"You don't have to do that. I'm good. I know how to handle these guys." Jake buckled Emma in her car seat. Those little fingers still gripped the small rubber bunny. Perfect size for her hands.

"I'm right behind you." She got in her car and waited.

He started the car and headed home.

A huff escaped his lips. His rearview mirror revealed Daria's squad car following close behind. He could defend himself. She'd been kind to him and looked all official in her uniform, but she was a cop, and the police didn't help Amanda when she filed a report about the threats. No one took her seriously. Was Daria one of the guilty parties? Who could he trust? No one.

Trust was a rare commodity and an endangered trait. Jake had trusted too much, especially on the battlefield, and it got his buddy Nolan killed. Nolan had insisted he could crawl unnoticed from the bunker and throw a grenade across the enemy line because he was smaller in stature than Jake was.

"Trust me. I've got this," he'd said. Jake had prayed for whatever good it did. The enemy shot him as he lifted his torso from the ground and threw the grenade. Successful throw, but seconds too late.

Jake wiped his hand across his mouth. Would he ever overcome the guilt of his friend's death? He glanced back at Emma. She'd thrown diapers, clothes and more little rubber animals out of the diaper bag and found her pink-and-white cup. Smart and self-sufficient. They just might get along.

"You found your cup, didn't you?" He smiled at her through the rearview mirror.

"Yes." She shook her head up and down, making her short black curls dance. "Cup." Her dark onyx eyes latched on to his eyes in the mirror and melted his heart.

There was no way around it. He had to take care of this tiny human and carry out his sister's wishes. Failure wasn't in his vocabulary. Somehow, he'd figure it out.

The shooter was another story. He preferred investigating on his own. Once he had proof, he'd present the evidence to the authorities. He'd begin by questioning Amanda's coworkers at the bank.

Jake turned into the driveway and pressed the remote. The garage door opened. Daria parked midway on the drive. He pulled the car into the garage and closed the door. His thoughts drifted back to the disarray of the house when he'd first arrived this morning. He'd considered calling the police and reporting the incident, but what would they do? They didn't protect his sister. At least he took pictures as proof the intruder had been there. Had he found what he was looking for? Jake didn't know, but he was certain he and Emma were now in their crosshairs.

Jake rolled his shoulders and popped his neck before he got out of the car and opened the back door to get Emma. He scooped up the tossed contents of the diaper bag and stuffed them back inside the bag. With her cup in one hand, hanging by the handle, and the white rubber bunny in the other, Emma's arms stretched out to him.

"Want you." Her legs kicked as he picked her up and her dainty arms wrapped around his neck.

So, this is what the love of a child feels like.

"You're the only one who does, kiddo." He patted her back, went inside and set her down. "Guess I need to open the front door. It would be rude to leave Daria sitting outside in the cold." He liked her, but he didn't want her telling him what to do and how to do it. He had his own way of tracking down the enemy.

"Door." Emma ran to the door and tapped it with one finger.

"Yep. You talk pretty good for one who's so little." He scooped her up with one arm, opened the wood door with the free hand and unlocked the security door. "Come on in."

"Thanks." Daria stepped inside, holding an iPad. "Brrr, it's getting colder. No doubt bad weather will set in later. I hear we have a chance for sleet and snow tonight."

"Don't plan on getting out." He fought the resentment welling up. If she'd gone after the guy who sped away when she'd first spotted him, there wouldn't have been a shooting, and this whole mess could be over and done with.

"Nice house. But what happened in here?" She walked into the living room, obviously looking the place over. "From what I remember, Amanda loved to decorate. Didn't matter what it was but this wasn't her style."

"I told you it got ransacked. Like I said, she left me everything. She'd always kept a clean house and fussed at me if I put my feet on her coffee table." Jake pointed to the navy leather couch. "Have a seat if you can find a spot. I still have cleaning to do after the intruders tossed everything."

"Ma-ma." Emma toddled down the hall, pointing to the master bedroom. "Ma-ma. Bed."

"Funny how the kid recognizes names." He watched Emma waddle up and down the hallway, then into the living room. She set her cup on the leather ottoman and pounded the rubber bunny next to it. The chair and ottoman were navy, too, and everything matched.

"She's so cute. I adore her dark hair and eyes." Daria turned and looked at him. "I'd like to meet your wife. Is she here? She doesn't need to be afraid. I'll have a police presence outside your home for a while."

Jake bit his tongue. He didn't want to be rude to his childhood friend and cause more friction between them. "Let me reiterate. I am a marine. I understand the dangers of the enemy. No disrespect to you or your occupation, but your department didn't help my sister, so I have a hard time trusting they will help me now. And for the record, I am not married, and I don't have a girlfriend."

Daria's eyebrows lifted. "Oh. I just assumed." She pointed to Emma.

"When I told you Amanda left me everything, she left me her only daughter, too. Emma is my niece."

"I see." Daria walked over to the fireplace and picked up a family photo from the mantel. "I'm still trying to figure out how I didn't know Amanda lived in Kimbleton. I should have figured it out. Better yet, I should have seen her around town." She put the photo back in place.

"You know, it shouldn't matter who calls for help, whether the person is a friend or an unknown. They should follow up on every death threat." Jake's comment came out a little more cynical than he intended.

She spun and propped her hands at her waist. "We take our jobs seriously. You, of all people, should know that and understand the law of the land and police jurisdictions. You have protocol in the military, and you had to abide by them. Now that you are home, you must consider who will care for Emma if you take the law into your own hands and kill someone or get yourself killed. I really am sorry for your loss, but let the police handle it."

Jake held back a smile. "You've gotten pretty feisty through the years."

"Stop. I'm serious." She shook her head.

"Why didn't you go to nursing school like you'd dreamed?" Jake studied Daria. It was nice to have an old friend still in his hometown, even if she was a little bossy.

"You're changing the subject." Daria closed her iPad. "I almost finished my nursing degree, but once I started clinicals and saw the number of people wounded from fights, gunshots, knives, overdoses, etc., I opted for the police department in hopes I could help stop some of these needless crimes. Why didn't you pursue football and become the quarterback you talked about? You were always good at sports."

"Somehow, after the war broke out, playing football seemed irrelevant. The desire to join the military and serve my country took priority. Guess God didn't want me to be involved with sports. Maybe I needed the discipline. I don't know." Jake pulled out his phone. "What's your number? I'll send you the pictures I took of the mess the intruders left. I've cleaned some of it up."

"You shouldn't have touched anything and called us immediately. Now you've contaminated the crime scene." She gave him her number and lifted her cell. "I'll take a few more pictures to add to the report."

"Go ahead." He scooped Emma into his arms and followed Daria through the house as she took pictures of the disarray in each room. "By the way, it's nice to see you again." He let his squirming niece slide from his arms to the floor.

"You, too, Jake." Daria returned to the living room. "I'll go finish my report in the car before I head back. If you need anything, you've got my number. I'm just a phone call away."

"Thanks, I appreciate it." Jake walked Daria toward the front door.

Bullets shattered the living room window. Emma screamed. Jake dived for Emma, pulled his weapon and covered her with his body. He held her like a football and inched back for better cover. "Are you okay?" he asked Daria.

She held her pistol in one hand and the radio clipped to her shoulder in the other as she rolled across the floor toward them. "Shots fired. Need backup."

TWO

Daria shielded Jake and Emma as more bullets pelted through the window. Glass from framed pictures on the opposite wall shot like daggers across the room with each hit. She inched her way to the side of a window and fired back.

Emma's cries filled the air. Poor baby. Daria prayed for the first time since her friend's death four years ago.

Dear Lord, I know I haven't reached out to You in a while, but please, help keep baby Emma safe.

It couldn't hurt to try, although Daria had a hard time trusting Him after her prayers had gone unanswered when Joni had her heart attack.

Jake rushed toward her. What was he doing?

"Stop. Get down." Daria threw her hand out toward him.

"You watch Emma while I go out the back door and scout out the shooters." Jake pushed Emma into her arms, then retrieved his pistol from his shoulder holster.

"Oh, no you don't. You stay put." Emma latched on to Daria and laid her head on her shoulder. "We're going to have to agree to disagree and work together. You be the trained marine, and I'll be the experienced police officer. Put our wisdom together and we might survive this attack. Help is on the way. It may take them a few minutes, considering how far out of town we are."

"I can get to them. Don't patronize me." His eyebrows lowered.

"I'm not, Jake. I'm trying to get you to work with me and not against me. Here in the States, it's my responsibility to protect you and Emma. I realize you are a well-trained soldier with many hidden talents. I don't doubt your abilities. Trust me and let me do my job."

"People earn trust, and I'm still assessing you." He eyed her and then backed off. A smile emerged as he lifted his eyebrows up and down. A gesture he did back in their school days when she was upset. "I remember you always babysitting and carrying a kid around in the neighborhood. You're good with babies. That's why you're the only one I trust to be near her right now."

"You are impossible." She held back her frustration at his bantering. "This is serious business. There's a shooter out there determined to take us out. It's nothing to joke and laugh about." Unbeknownst to him, she was still assessing him, too. He seemed innocent enough, but his resistance to her authority would have to stop.

"You're right." He leaned close to the window and pushed the curtain aside. "I still could creep up on them."

Daria rolled her eyes. She raised up just enough to peer out of the broken window and not expose Emma. "There are two people over there, running through the woods. Did you see movement in those bushes? Not sure if it's another shooter or an animal."

"Car doors slammed." Jake pointed. "There, in the distance. Do you see that black car? I can't figure out the make or model through all the foliage. Over there, a third shooter running to the car."

Tires squealed as the car sped away. Daria radioed the update.

She leaned against the wall with Emma still hanging on and sucking on two of her fingers. Emma held her other hand out to Jake. He took her and held her against his chest.

"Everything's going to be okay. Uncle Jake won't let anything happen to you." He kissed the top of her head and smoothed her hair.

Who knew this tough military man could be so gentle? Those biceps bulged, and Emma rested securely in his arms between his broad shoulders. The transformation in Jake's demeanor warmed Daria's heart.

"What exactly did Amanda and your brother-in-law do for a living? Any idea who has a vendetta against you?"

"No clue." Jake paced, holding a sleepy baby. "Tom was an attorney in Los Angeles. He transferred to Kimbleton and set up a virtual office so Amanda could be closer to Dad and Mom after they retired and moved back. Amanda worked at the Crow's Ridge Bank across the county line for a couple of years. She advanced from teller to auditor in a short time."

"Do you think the threats came from someone at work?" Daria made notes on her iPad.

"Last time we talked, she didn't mention the bank. Said she was looking for a more reputable job. I couldn't help but question her word choice. Reputable. Wouldn't her position at the bank meet that criterion?" He placed the sleeping Emma on the couch and put pillows around her.

"One would think so." Daria followed him and gazed down at Emma's innocence. Who would want to hurt either of them? He hadn't been in town long, and someone was already gunning for him.

Her eyes shifted to Jake. "I'm here to help. I'll do what I can to find out what happened to Amanda and Tom, and who is behind these shootings. I'll locate your sister's file and figure out where the investigation trail stopped."

"You're not doing this alone. These people don't care who they eliminate as long as they get what they want." He stepped back over to the window and looked out. "The cops are here." He looked back at Daria. "*More* cops are here."

"My coworkers can help figure this out." She approached the front door and opened it at their knock, then introduced everyone. "Cramer, McDaniel, this is Jake Fisher, a friend from the past. The sleeping beauty on the couch is Emma, Jake's niece." She explained the situation.

"She's eighteen months old and shouldn't be in the middle of this mess." Jake shook hands with them. "Any idea if the shooters were caught?"

"Officers are involved in a chase as we speak. We will keep you updated. Anyone hurt?" Cramer made notes on a little spiral notepad he pulled from his shirt pocket.

"The shattering glass and loud shooting frightened Emma, but there are no injuries. Jake calmed Emma's cries, and she finally drifted off to sleep."

The officers walked around in the living room inspecting the damage. They paused in front of Emma.

McDaniel tightened his jaw, while Cramer pressed his lips together. After working with them for several years, Daria recognized the anger stirring inside them over a baby being amid the danger or possibly being a target. An even more unreasonable thought.

"Did you see the shooter?" Cramer walked over to the broken window. "How many were there?"

"Best we could—"

"Three," Jake interrupted and squared his shoulders. "They had a black car waiting on the road over there." He pointed.

Heat rose in Daria's cheeks. He'd cut her off while she was giving the report to her coworkers. *Control your temper. Breathe.*

"The forest was too thick to get a description of the shooters." Daria stared at Jake. Was she being unreasonable, or was he being disrespectful? She'd let it go this time.

"They did a number on the windows and walls," McDaniel said. "This is now a crime scene." He turned and faced Daria. "They will have to stay somewhere else for a few days."

"This is my property and we're not leaving. I'll board up the windows and clean up the glass. Emma needs to be in her familiar surroundings. I've got this covered." Jake pushed his shoulders back with his legs slightly apart and his hands behind his back like the military "at ease" stance.

Daria noted his body language and his readiness to argue. "Jake, you should know a crime scene is off-limits to everyone except authorized personnel. I understand your position and your ability to face these shooters, but the thing you must consider is Emma's safety and her vulnerability for emotional trauma should anything else happen. You have a baby to consider now."

The hardness in his face relaxed. "I guess you're right. My thinking is still in military mode. This was my sister's house, and I don't want any more destruction to happen to it."

"After you replenish Emma's diaper bag, I'll take it with me to the car while you get a few necessities, then we'll go to the station. Maybe we can figure things out from there." Daria pointed to Jake. "I'll pull my squad car close to the garage door in case someone's still lurking."

"We will set up the crime scene tape," McDaniel said. "Two squad cars will escort you to the station."

"Perfect. Thanks." Daria turned to Jake. "Grab some more diapers, changes of clothes and a couple of blankets. Be sure to bring some snacks and whatever else she needs."

Good thing she'd had experience babysitting. She dreamed of having a family of her own one day and becoming a stay-at-home mom.

She spun and ran into Jake. He grabbed her shoulders and kept her from falling. A tingling shot across her shoulders at his touch—a warm sensation she'd never experienced.

"Are you okay?" Jake's dark eyes bore into hers.

His firm grip made her feel safe. Wasn't that backward? She was the authority figure. She was supposed to keep him safe. Who was protecting whom here?

"Yes. Did you get the food items and some things for yourself?" She pulled away from his hold and walked past him. "I'm going to the car. Don't linger when you come out. I don't want anyone's crosshairs on you or Emma."

"Got it." His expression grew solemn. "We'll be waiting."

Daria grabbed the diaper bag. She spotted the tiny rubber bunny still on the ottoman beside Emma's cup. She tossed them both into the bag. Cramer and McDaniel stepped inside.

"Time to go," McDaniel said.

"I moved the baby's car seat to your vehicle." Cramer straightened his uniform shirt.

"Thanks. I hadn't thought about that. Grab those two backpacks for me. Jake doesn't need to be bogged down with baggage getting in the car. He needs to focus on Emma." Daria rushed out the front door to her car. She popped the trunk and her coworkers placed the rest of the baggage inside, then slammed it closed.

She rolled forward and the car hobbled badly. She got out and checked her tires. Sure enough, her back tires were flat. She ran back inside.

"What is it?" McDaniel met her at the entrance.

"Looks like someone slashed my back tires." Goose bumps rushed over her arms, and it wasn't the chilly winter wind. Had the shooters cut them before they showered them with bullets and then ran or were there more gunmen hiding in the forest, waiting for their next move?

Jake appeared from the kitchen, holding a sleepy Emma. "We can take my car. It's in the garage where we're better protected loading up. I spotted an extra car seat over in the far corner if you want to grab that one."

"Perfect. Cramer, can you grab the diaper bag from my back floorboard? McDaniel, do you mind getting the backpacks from my trunk? I don't have a good feeling about this. Stay alert." Daria rushed into the garage and located the car seat. She secured it in place, since the other one was now in her disabled vehicle.

Cramer and McDaniel entered through the front door and met her in the closed garage. Daria took the diaper bag and placed it on the floor of the back seat.

Jake came out carrying his niece. His size made her look so tiny. He buckled her in. She whined. He gave her the rubber rabbit and her cup. She gripped the bunny and tucked it up under her chin like she was hugging it and drifted off to sleep.

"I'll drive," she said and held her hand out for the keys.

"I don't think so." Jake hopped into the driver's seat. "Besides, should anything happen, you need to be free to focus."

"I'm not arguing. Let's get out of here, quick." Daria sat on the passenger side and buckled up. She radioed the waiting squad cars and updated them on the vehicle switch.

The garage door opened. Jake backed out and drove around Daria's squad car faster than she expected. The waiting squad cars were in position. One at the end of the driveway and one behind them.

"How fast do you want me to drive?" Jake's eyes cut over to her eyes.

"How important is Emma's and your life? We don't know if there's another shooter hiding in the forest. Stay on the tail of the lead squad car."

* * *

Jake rode the bumper of the car in front of them, as Daria instructed. He checked his rearview mirror and passing vehicles for suspicious activity. All seemed clear. His muscles tensed at the attempts on his and Emma's lives since he'd arrived home. He mulled over the sequence of events. Amanda must have hit a nerve with someone, but she'd never been a troublemaker. She was the introvert in the family. Quiet and meek. Everyone loved her. At least, he thought so.

Who knew Daria would still be in Kimbleton, and had become a law enforcement officer rather than a nurse? It looked like she'd done well for herself as a cop and was insistent on maintaining the law in the area. A sparkle had shone in her eyes when he'd smiled and made his eyebrows dance. Timing was off, but after all these years, he could still read her mood by making eye contact. She was none too happy with him for interrupting her in front of her coworkers. He'd have to tone down his extrovert outbursts.

"Are you cold?" Jake noted Daria with her arms crossed. "The sun's going down, and the temperature is dropping."

"I'm not worried about me. It could be a little cool for Emma, though." She reached over and tucked the soft blanket around the baby's sleeping body. "There. That's better."

Jake turned up the heat and adjusted the air vents to blow more toward the back. Daria turned the vent by the window toward herself. Just as he thought, she was cold, too. She never was one to complain. Guess that's why they got along so well when they were kids. Now she'd become outspoken and authoritative. Nice change.

He glanced back at Emma. His heart hitched at her innocence. She had his sister's features and some of her personality. Could he care for her like Amanda did? Probably not. He wasn't the mom. One thing he could do was protect and love her. He would tell her stories of her parents, so she'd never forget them. Amanda would like that.

They pulled into the police station just as a police officer hung a Christmas wreath on the double glass doors. He parked and got out of the car.

"I'll get Emma." He looked at Daria over the top of the car. "Will you grab the diaper bag?"

Daria didn't waste any time getting the bag and meeting him on the driver's side. He lifted the light-weight child into his arms. Her head popped up. Eyes wide. Daria raised the hood of Emma's coat over her head to keep the chilly wind off her face. Emma tossed it off with her hand.

"Let's get inside." Daria pointed to the doors.

The officers who'd escorted them on the road entered behind them. A fresh scent of pine hit Jake's nostrils and sent him searching for the source. There it was. A live Christmas tree in the corner of the entry, decorated for the season. The smell reminded him of the times he went hunting with his dad and they walked through patches of pine trees.

Daria sniffed the air and smiled. "Mmm, what smells so good in here?" Daria glanced over at the tree and smiled. "With everything we see in this line of work, it's nice to have a little festivity. I hope we can solve this case soon so you and Emma can try to have a normal holiday."

"Yeah, best I remember, you always thought everyone should enjoy the holidays as much as you." Jake followed her down the long hallway. "It's too much work putting a tree up, decorating, then having to take it all down and pack it up, all within a month. Don't get me wrong. I'm all about the food and desserts at this time of year." He patted his stomach with his free hand. "I'll think about the tree. Too much going on right now. She won't know the difference."

"You used to put away a lot of food in that hollow leg. As far as a tree, she may not be old enough to understand Christmas, but she'd be captivated by all the twinkling lights. Making memories is super special. She'll love you even more for taking pictures. Right now, we have more important matters to take care of." She opened a door and showed Jake inside.

"Nice big room." He pulled out a rolling leather chair and sat down, placing Emma on his knee. "That's a huge picture window. You could sit in the warmth and watch the city from here."

"I'll be right back." Daria closed the door behind her.

Emma straightened her legs and scooted off his lap, then took off running around the table. She stopped at a cabinet set up as a coffee station with a water dispenser.

"Bite." She pointed to the sugar canister. "Cup." She toddled to the picture window. The cold weather fogged the lower portion as darkness descended over the town. Emma pressed her hand on the glass while her nose and forehead butted against it. Everywhere she touched left its mark. She slapped at the foggy places and giggled.

"Wish I had all that energy." Jake admired her cuteness. So many of her mannerisms reminded him of his sister. His heart sank. If only Amanda were here. "I'll find the ones responsible for your death if it's the last thing I do."

"What's the last thing you'll do?" Daria had returned to the room with a laptop in her hand.

"I was thinking out loud." He turned his swivel chair to face the oval-shaped wood table. "I'll find the killer with your help, of course."

Daria's eyes latched on to his eyes for a moment. He could tell she was evaluating his statement. She walked over, pulled the floor-length gray curtains across the large window, returned and sat in the chair next to him. "I need your full report on everything. When you arrived, when things started happening, the break-ins, the shooting, etc., etc. Had you received threatening calls or suspicious mail?"

"None of that. Only the break-in." The interview was short since there wasn't much to report. Daria's fingers slid across the keyboard as she typed. No wedding band, not even an indent of a ring ever being on her finger.

"Here it is. Took me a minute, but I found it." She clicked on the icon and the document opened. "Looks like someone placed it in the wrong electronic folder."

"On purpose?" Jake's pulse increased.

"No, not at all. I suppose it was just a clerical error." She cleared her throat. "I'll let you read your sister's comments."

Jake leaned toward the small screen and read out loud, "'I've received a couple of death threats in my personal email, and I believe I'm being followed. My family and I need protection. There are questionable things going on, but I cannot give names because I don't know who to trust. They know what I've done.'"

"What did she do?" Daria sat back in her chair.

Emma slapped at one of the other leather chairs. It turned. Her smiles and jabbers touched Jake's heart. She gripped the chair and turned it in circles until she tripped over her own foot. She pushed up and toddled over to her diaper bag sitting on the floor, then plopped down beside it. Jake monitored her while she tossed diapers out of the bag and pulled out several rubber animals from the bottom. She still held the little bunny but lined up the rest of the rubber farm animals with her other hand, then knocked them over and giggled.

"I have no clue what Amanda meant. I'm almost certain it's something to do with her bank job. Why else would she look for another job?" Jake rubbed his chin. "Why didn't the police take her seriously?"

"It says they sent an officer out to her house and looked around." Daria squinted at the report and looked at him. "It also says that there wasn't enough information to go on, and they couldn't do anything unless something else happened."

"Like death? That's some protection." Jake stood so fast his chair almost fell over. "So, Amanda and Tom are dead because 'something' had to happen. That's hogwash." Heat pulsated in his face, and he bit back his emotions. He paced. Emma ran over and grabbed his leg.

He looked down at her, stopped and picked her up, burying his face in her little neck.

Daria walked over to him and placed her hand on his arm. "I'm sorry."

"Don't even go there." His voice rose louder than he meant. He blew out several huffs. "The police got what they wanted and then ruled it an 'accident.' Did anyone investigate or did they assume?"

"I'm sure they did a thorough investigation. I was on vacation when it happened. That's why I didn't know anything about it. I will check into it and see what their findings were." She patted his arm gently, then smoothed her finger across Emma's cheek. "I'll go to the bank tomorrow and question the employees."

"I'm going with you." Jake tightened his lips. He wanted to see these people face-to-face and look them in the eyes.

THREE

Daria wasn't about to tell Jake he couldn't go to the bank with her. The hurt on his face pricked her heart. Investigating with a baby in tow wasn't the best idea, but Jake wasn't about to let her out of his sight. She'd have to give it some serious thought.

"We can't stay at the station all night. Emma needs a comfortable, warm place to sleep. Is that big hotel I remember still at the foothills of the Ozark National Forest?" He held Emma like a football again while he picked up the diapers and toys and stuffed them back into the diaper bag.

"It's still there. They've done some remodeling in the past ten years. It's nice." Daria breathed a sigh of relief. At least he didn't ask to be taken home. "I'll get your car and pull up at the back door. When you walk out of the conference room, turn right, then left in the first hallway. The exit is straight ahead. I'll meet you there."

"Got it." Jake adjusted his hold on Emma, handed the keys over to Daria and tossed the diaper bag over his opposite shoulder.

Daria eyed him before she left the room. She compared him to a gorilla carrying a baby chick. His height and strong build, holding a petite baby, looked awkward, but he managed just fine. Once he got used to caring for her, he'd be a great substitute dad.

She stepped out into the cold and reported their destination to Lieutenant Jeffers. Sleet bounced off her face and her breath fogged. It was going to be a cold, treacherous night for anyone on the streets. She slid into Jake's car and eased to the back door of the station. Jake stepped out and covered Emma's head until he reached the car. She clung to him and didn't want in her car seat. He talked in a smooth tone and got her buckled in.

Good job.

"Remind me of how far that hotel is from here." He rubbed his hands together. "What is the temperature?"

"Not sure exactly, but I think it's somewhere around nineteen degrees." She pulled onto the street.

Thank You, God. Traffic has thinned to minimal cars. Did I just whisper a prayer?

Vacationers had already retreated to their hotels and condominiums. Who would want to walk the town in the sleet and snow?

"Oh, the hotel is about twenty minutes from here. It's about five minutes from the Marketplace Grocery where the road forks and narrows from four lanes to two." She rolled to a stop at a red light. "By the way, this is a nice SUV."

"Not my choice of vehicles, but I can't complain. Amanda had her own taste in things." His tone was solemn. "I'd get a Mustang or a motorcycle."

"I can see you with one of those. Of course, I've known some girls who like motorcycles too." She rolled through the green light and watched the rearview mirror. The headlights of the cars behind them were a distance away. Safe so far.

"What about you? What's your preference?" Jake shifted his body and faced her.

His gaze made her cheeks warm. Was she blushing? Glad it was dark outside.

"I have a Jeep. Its off-road capabilities are excellent for the area." She smiled, proud to announce her choice of vehicles in the Ozarks.

"Not too bad. I figured you would drive a midsize car or even a Volkswagen."

"Are you serious?" She snickered. "I like those, too, but I still like the Jeep best. The hotel is just ahead."

His laughter took her back to when they were kids. They'd rolled down grassy hills every chance they had. Only, one hill they'd selected dropped them about three feet, and they'd bumped into each other. They'd howled out belly laughs until their sides hurt. The only difference now was his masculine build and his deep voice.

Bright lights lit up the portico. Fake snow framed each glass door and window to the entrance. An extra-large Christmas welcome mat lay in front of the double glass doors.

She pulled up and unbuckled her seatbelt. "Stay here. I'll get the room."

The registration desk looked cheerful with all the festive decor. She took in a deep sniff of the pine aroma from the live Christmas tree. A small gold bell sat on the counter. Daria rang it twice.

Her young friend Shelby, whom she'd been mentoring and had helped financially a few times, stepped out of the office behind the desk wearing sunglasses.

"Daria, uh, it's good to see you." She picked up a pen and tapped the counter nervously. "How can I help you?"

"Are you okay? You're red around your eyebrow."

"Another migraine. I've been rubbing my forehead and eyebrows because the light hurts my eyes." Shelby tapped on the computer. "What can I do for you?"

"I'm sorry you're not feeling well. I need a room for a friend and his baby." Daria looked around. Something seemed off. "Are you sure you're okay? You looked stressed."

Shelby smirked. "Oh, you know me. I'm always stressed. No worries, though." She clicked on the computer. "How about the fourth floor? It's nice and spacious. I can give you the police discount."

"Perfect." Daria still wasn't sure about Shelby's headache. It must be so hard to work with the constant pounding. Bless her heart, she'd had a rough time since her parents' accidental death a few years back. "It's Christmas. Time to de-stress and have fun." Daria backed away and headed outside.

She walked out of the automatic doors, happy she'd secured a room on the highest floor possible. She opened the back door of the car and reached in for Emma. Jake stepped out and grabbed the diaper bag.

"Want to get the bags from the trunk?" Daria shuffled Emma in her arms and opened the trunk. Jake tossed the handles of his bags over his shoulder. A big yawn covered Emma's face. Poor baby. She didn't deserve to be in this situation.

Jake took a sniff as they walked through the entry. "Smells like the forest."

They stepped into the elevator. Jake's expression changed.

"What's wrong? I got you a room on the top floor with a beautiful view." She studied him. "No one can reach you easily up there."

"I'm not comfortable on the top floor. There are limited escape routes this high up." His irritated tone punched her in the gut.

"Jake, you're on US soil, not in Afghanistan. You're not being reasonable." She focused on her tone and kept her temper in check. If he kept pushing her buttons, she'd have to walk away rather than lose it.

"I'm just saying. You haven't been where I have, so your perception is going to differ from mine." He took Emma and patted her on the back. The bags dropped from his shoulder and hung on his arm. "I'll stay this time, but I'd like to be moved to the bottom floor tomorrow."

"Okay. I had good intentions, but you're right. My thoughts are not your thoughts."

Hmm, did I just quote the Bible?

Daria's spirits dropped as disappointment set in. She thought she'd done well, maybe even impressed him, considering the season and all the tourists piling in for the Christmas holidays. She admired his tenacity. His take-charge demeanor and determination were commendable, but she placed the responsibility on herself to protect them regardless of his attitude or difference of opinion.

She slid the room key into the slot and the door opened. Daria took the diaper bag from Jake and set it and the two backpacks on the floor, while Jake put sleepy Emma on the bed in the second bedroom. A whimper came from the room but quickly grew silent.

"I'm not sure if she'll go back to sleep, but for now, I've got pillows around her. She's got her sippy cup and that silly rubber toy." Jake took off his jacket and rubbed the top of his head. "I appreciate all of your help. You've been tremendous in seeing to our safety and needs. I can take it from here. You should go home and get some rest, so you'll be ready for work tomorrow."

"In case you don't remember how things work here in the US, I *am* at work. Protecting you and Emma is my job right now." She expected a rebuttal, but he walked away.

His body language told her he wasn't happy. She'd already figured out that he resented her thinking she had to protect him. She got it. Really. He stood tall, in fact, a little more than a head taller than her. His driver's license stated his height was six foot two. He was broad shouldered, stout and, according to him, well educated in his military field. Best she remembered, he'd made honor roll throughout school, so he was very intelligent. His giving in to her was probably a little demeaning to his ego.

He placed the diaper bag on the table, unpacked it and rearranged its contents, including the little rubber toys. He tapped the bottom of the bag. "This is a quality, well-made bag. The bottom of it is solid. My sister probably paid a high price for it. Leave it to her to get the best for her baby."

"That's nice." Daria wanted to smooth things over with Jake before she left. She approached the opposite side of the table from where he stood.

"I never asked how your parents are doing. I know you said earlier they'd retired and moved back to Kimbleton, but physically could not keep Emma." She stuck her hands in her jacket pockets.

He placed two small cans of apple juice in a side pocket of the diaper bag, then put an empty sippy cup and the remaining diapers inside the bag. "They are up in years. Dad uses a walker and Mom thinks she's steady enough to use a cane. Honestly, they need to be in a nursing home, but neither will even consider it. Can't say that I blame them. I wouldn't want to lose my independence, either. Now that I'm home, I'll have to keep an eye on them."

"That's an enormous responsibility. My parents are still active and doing well. I don't know what I'll do when they need 24-7 care."

He stopped busying himself and looked at her with a serious but soft expression.

"You've really changed, for the better, I mean. You're authoritative, fearless and good at your job." He adjusted his stance. "I'm proud of you for outgrowing your shyness and squeamish personality that I remember from school."

She held his gaze while her insides did flips. Fearless would not be how she'd describe herself, because right then she was terrified of his sincere compliments. How long had it been since someone complimented her so deeply? She tried not to swallow hard. He would notice. Good thing her hands were in her pockets. She could feel the sweat in her palms.

"Thank you, Jake. I don't know what to say. I'm glad you're back in Kimbleton. Just sorry for the reason that brought you here. I don't doubt for one minute you can't take care of yourself and Emma. I see you as strong and fully capable. The only drawback is my boss assigned me to watch after your safety. It's not a matter of your weakness. You're not weak by any means. It's my job and I must follow through, and, I might add, I'm glad he assigned me. We understand each other." She turned. "I should go and let you get some rest. I've said too much."

She placed her hand on the doorknob. His long arm reached ahead of her and pulled the door open. For a millisecond, his warm breath hit her neck. She bit her lip and stepped into the hallway.

I can't let him get to me. We're friends. That's it. Friends.

She cleared her throat. "You can never be too safe. Please lock and deadbolt your door. I don't trust anyone right now."

She had to get away before gushy words started spilling from her lips. Had Jake sensed the same connection she had? Her heart fluttered every time his deep brown eyes zeroed in on her. She shook it off. Mixing police work with personal feelings wasn't allowed in the department.

Jake leaned on the doorjamb and watched Daria walk away. He'd stared into her brown eyes, and her light brown hair glistened in the hall light. His breath hitched. For an instant, he'd wanted to kiss her. Where had that come from? What was he thinking? They'd only reconnected a few hours ago.

She stopped at the elevator and pushed the button.

"Good night. See you in the morning." Jake nodded.

The elevator door opened. "Rest well." She stepped in and the door closed.

He stared down the hall. What just happened? He wasn't looking for a relationship, even if they were old friends. She was a cop. There was someone after him and Emma. He stepped inside the room and locked the door.

He rubbed both hands over his face, then made his way to the brown couch. His weary body sank into the fabric's softness. Nothing like the beds he'd slept on overseas. It had been a long day escaping the mysterious US enemy. Daria, the one girl he'd always cared for and thought about, was back in his life. He'd have to keep her at arm's length and not get involved with her. He had Emma to focus on and caring for her would be a full-time job.

Jake huffed. He needed to check on Emma, change her diaper and put her warm, footed pajamas on her before he relaxed too much and fell asleep. He pushed to his feet and eased into the room where she slept. She'd rolled over and her little rear stuck in the air.

He slowly took her coat off, something he should have done earlier before he laid her down, carefully placed her onto her back and proceeded to change her diaper and clothes. She whimpered. He gave her the sippy cup and covered her up with a fluffy pink blanket. One of her hands held the cup handle and the other hand lightly patted her head and twirled hair between her fingers. She turned on her side and her eyes closed.

He yawned and stretched his arms into the air before going to the master bedroom. A hot shower sounded good. Fancy hotels always had nice decor, but this one had an enormous bathroom with white robes hanging on the back of the door, monogrammed hand soap, even a television on the wall opposite the tub. Who wanted to spend that much time in the bathroom?

A slight thump caught his attention. Had Emma fallen off the bed? His first thought was to rush into the room, but instinct said to wait. He listened. She wasn't crying. Something felt off. He stepped out of the shower and wrapped a towel around his lower body. Steam from his hot shower fogged up the mirror.

His pistol lay on the chest. He grabbed it and plastered himself against the bedroom wall by the door and eased around enough to see into the living room. No movement. His eyes squinted as he studied every item in the room. Wait. The diaper bag had fallen off the table, and Emma's extra sippy cup was under the chair.

He straightened, moved quietly to Emma's room and glanced inside. She looked undisturbed and peaceful. Jake breathed a satisfied breath, even though his heart pounded from the adrenaline rush. He returned to the dining area, retrieved the diaper bag and cup and placed them in the chair. Then he returned to his room, redressed and repacked his bag. With uncertainty hanging in the air, he'd sleep fully clothed as he'd done in Afghanistan, ready to bolt if necessary. His pistol remained in his holster as he mounted it around his shoulder.

The bright-colored geometric bedspread wasn't his style, but who cared? It was a bed. He laid across the firm mattress and stared at the ceiling. He reminisced about fun times with his sister and going deer hunting with Tom. He was a great brother-in-law, and he made Amanda happy. They'd been so excited about her pregnancy. Jake had spoken to her many times over the phone and could hear the joy in her voice. He wiped the wetness from his eyes, thankful no one was there to see a marine crying.

"Maa…ma, Maa…ma." Emma's crying shot him to his feet.

He ran to her room. She sat in the middle of the bed, rubbing her closed eyes. Jake picked her up, along with her cup and rabbit, and went into the kitchen. He couldn't decide what to give her. Milk or apple juice? Since he wasn't a fan of milk, he filled the cup with the juice. She reached for it before he'd secured the lid. When he pulled it away to pop the lid on, she screamed loudly.

"Whoa, I'm sorry, but I had to put the lid on good or we'd both have apple juice all over us. Here. You're okay." He handed her the cup, patted her back and paced with her. Her crying finally stopped. "Who knew you could turn a cup upside down and it wouldn't drip? What will they think of next?"

Jake thought he heard a faint noise but after listening for a few seconds and hearing only silence, he shook his head and went back into the living room. "I'm a little jumpy tonight, but we are in a hotel. Maybe we can relax a bit. What do you think, little girl?" He laid his head gently against his niece's soft curls. "You sleep, short ribs. I've got you."

She drank from the dripless cup with her eyes closed. He slumped on the couch, holding her against his chest. Her breathing grew deeper, with the cup curled in her hand against her side. He admired her tiny features before he closed his eyes. A dull headache emerged and sleep failed him.

His marine security thinking shifted to planning an escape route should he need it. Top floors of hotels are normally nice with an incredible view, as Daria had pointed out. Why was he so uptight about it? Too many places during the war blew up, leaving people trapped under all the debris. Daria only wanted them to have the best care possible. Had he been too hard on her?

He looked around the semidark room. A dim night-light from the kitchen cast a haze across the ceiling. Jake blinked. He must be more exhausted than he thought. Were his eyes blurry?

Funny, he hadn't noticed the growing fog a little while ago. Had the temperature dropped so much outside that he didn't have the heat turned up enough? What sense did that make?

"What's going on?" He grew suspicious.

The room was a comfortable temperature, but curiosity got the best of him. He slid Emma onto the couch and scooted off. She wiggled for a second but settled down. Jake stood and listened. What was that light hissing sound and that slight chemical odor? He went into the kitchen and turned on the range hood light.

"Where is this haze coming from?" The hair on his neck bristled and investigative mode kicked in. He pulled out his phone, turned on the flashlight app to keep from waking Emma, and walked into the living room. The small light confirmed his suspicions. A thin cloud had formed across the ceiling and more of the substance stirred with his movement. The odor grew stronger as the cloud began filling the room.

His eyes landed on the pilot light of the gas fire-place. A sudden surge of adrenaline shot through him. He coughed. The thump he'd heard earlier wasn't the diaper bag at all. Their location had been compromised. He scooped Emma up, still wrapped in her blanket, grabbed their coats and his bags and rushed out into the hall, which was free of the cloudy haze. More con-firmation something was amiss.

No way would he use the elevator. He wasn't about to get trapped between floors. A lighted sign hung above a door at the end of the hall. Stairs. He ran and thrust the door open. Cold, fresh air hit him in the face. Or-dinarily, he'd take three steps at a time or even jump from level to level, but with Emma in his arms, he'd best be sure-footed.

His feet moved almost at lightning speed. Thank-fully, the staircase was lit with security lights. "Third floor. Two more."

"Second floor, finally first floor." He bolted through the door and rushed down the hall toward the check-in desk. He paused, but no one was there. He exited through the automatic doors. This time frigid air blasted him, and a chill rushed over him like a splash of icy water. He hadn't taken the time to put on a coat, and he'd failed to put Emma's coat on her.

"Lord, which way do we go?" He paused and studied the cars in the parking lot. "Is that my car? Did Daria not leave, or did someone give her a ride?"

Jake checked for ice on the asphalt before picking up the pace. He headed for his car, noting a squad car had parked beside it. Daria jumped out of the squad car.

"What are you doing out here in the middle of the

night? It's freezing." She opened the back door for him to buckle Emma into the car seat. Emma rubbed her eyes and whimpered until her cup met her lips.

"Watch her while I go back to find the hotel staff so they can warn others to evacuate. There's a gas leak in my room and everyone needs to get out before it explodes." Jake turned to run back inside. "I paused to report the leak to the person at the front desk but no one was there and I didn't see a fire alarm pull station anywhere."

"No, don't," Daria said as she grabbed his arm. "Shelby should have been in there. I'll call for backup." She released her hold on him and notified the authorities on her shoulder radio. "What happened?"

"Get in and I'll explain." Jake opened his passenger door and got in. He shivered and placed his hands in front of the heat vents. Daria slid behind the steering wheel and gave him a questioning look.

Boom.

Flames burst through a top-floor window and glass rained down into the parking lot. He shot a look at Daria, and her widened eyes said it all. The blast wasn't an accident.

"They found us." He leaned forward and stared at the red, orange, and blue flames curling out of the window.

"How?" Daria called 911, then turned toward him. "Tell me what happened."

"I noticed a haze in the living room, so I got up to check it out. The air had a faint smell of insecticide. I started coughing and felt like I was suffocating. My head pounded. Emma was just below the fog, but her little body couldn't have handled much of it." He took in a deep breath, realizing he was talking fast. "That's when I grabbed her and our bags and ran down the stairs."

"I don't get it." Daria looked back at Emma. "No one knew where you were staying except my lieutenant and my friend Shelby. Come to think of it, she acted nervous while I made your reservation."

"She could have been threatened." Jake was certain that's what happened. His stalker had probably hid in her office.

A fire truck and ambulance pulled into the parking lot. Daria stepped out of Jake's car and approached the paramedics. She pointed at him, sitting in the car. They got their gear and walked toward him.

Firefighters jumped from the trucks, pulled hoses and hooked up to the water hydrant, while others grabbed their tools and ran toward the building. Huge streams of water shot through the air to the windows of the blazing room.

Daria moved around, meeting up with the squad cars as they pulled into the parking lot.

Other hotel patrons were escorted out of the blazing hotel wrapped in bed linens and blankets. Some were barefooted and shivering. Firefighters ushered them a safe distance away from danger. In a moment's time, a yellow school bus rolled onto the parking lot. Police officers sent the people to the bus to get out of the cold.

Thoughtful move.

A paramedic opened Jake's car door. "Sir, are you okay? The officer said you'd breathed some fumes. Tell me what happened."

Jake coughed, then cut his eyes to Daria out in the parking lot. She looked back at him. He was fine. Still coughing some, but okay. He explained the situation again. "Check my eighteen-month-old niece first. She's in the back."

"Yes, sir." He yelled at another medic as he opened the back door. "Grab me a child's mask."

The paramedic ran toward them with a small plastic bag containing a mask. The guy ripped it open and hooked it up before placing the mask over Emma's nose and mouth. She slapped at it, shook her head then started screaming. Her small hands tried to get it off, but the medic held it in place.

"Should I hold her to keep her from screaming?" Jake couldn't stand hearing her crying so hard.

"With her screaming like this, she's taking in more of the oxygen with every deep breath, which is good. Give her a couple of minutes and she should be fine."

The second medic placed a mask over Jake's mouth and nose. "Breathe in this oxygen for a few minutes. You probably breathed in more of the gas than the baby."

Jake coughed a few times. The cough urges grew farther apart until they finally stopped. He took off the mask and handed it back. "I think I'm good now. Thanks."

The paramedic let Emma pull off her mask. She threw it on the floor. Her red eyes and snotty nose were proof she didn't approve of them. She reached for Jake. He hopped out and pulled her from the car. Her coat lay on the floor along with her diaper bag.

Jake sat on the edge of the back seat with the door open. He put Emma's coat on her and rewrapped her with the blanket. A funny-shaped cloth hung halfway out of the bag. Jake wiped her face and nose. She screamed again, pushed his hand away and laid her head on his shoulder.

Such dainty arms wrapped around his neck calmed his jittery nerves. Protective mode for his sister's baby, now his baby, intensified. Such innocence, totally dependent on him, became a reality.

Jake shivered in the cold. His coat lay on the back floorboard, too, but he hadn't had time to put it on. Temperatures were much colder than earlier and small snowflakes hit his face. Emma had to be cold, too. He held her close, stepped inside the front seat and turned up the heat. She dropped her cup and put two fingers in her mouth, then stilled. He caught the cup before it landed in his lap.

Daria walked across the parking lot toward the car. Her breath fogged in the snowy night air. She'd worn her coat and gloves. Her nose was red. Just the sight of her returning to them set him at ease. The calming effect of her presence frustrated him. He couldn't get involved, even though his feelings for his childhood friend grew stronger. He had a kid to raise.

Smoke boiled into the night sky while firefighters fought the inferno. If he'd hesitated a minute longer, he and Emma wouldn't have made it. If he'd slowed his pace and walked down those stairs, they wouldn't have made it.

God, only You could have timed our escape that perfectly and saved us. I don't know why You didn't save Amanda and Tom, but please save anyone who is still in that hotel.

Daria hopped in the driver's side and shut the door. "Oh, it's nice and toasty in here." She took her gloves off and sat back. Her glance toward the squad car parked beside them and her solemn expression told him something was up.

"What's going on? You look upset." He shifted in the seat, still holding Emma.

"Personal stuff." She pushed a loose strand of hair out of her face. "I don't know how they knew where you were. I spotted a man sneaking around, a man who looked kind of sketchy. He stood at the corner of the hotel. I monitored him while talking to my lieutenant, Nolan Jeffers, but when you came out, the man ran into the forest. If I had questioned him when he appeared, maybe I could have gathered information and prevented the fire."

"You don't know he was involved." Jake reached over and took her hand. "Besides, at that point, there was nothing you could have done to stop the explosion. It's not your fault. Somehow, they knew our location and which room we were in."

FOUR

Daria gasped and her heart rate increased at the thought of her young friend who worked inside the hotel. She jerked her hand from Jake's hold. "Did you say you didn't see Shelby on your way out? She works the registration desk."

"No. Since no one was there, I kept running."

An uneasiness settled in her gut. Shelby should have been among the crowd or in the bus. Daria slid her gloves back on. "I'll be back."

She rushed through the crowd and checked the bus. No sign of her friend. Daria ran carefully on the icy parking lot toward the hotel.

A firefighter stopped her in the parking lot. "Officer, you can't go inside. It's not safe."

"I understand, but I need to check on the girl who runs the front desk. Her name is Shelby. She was there a little while ago." Daria pointed to the hotel. "Would you, please, have someone check the registration desk?"

He turned toward the fire truck. "Rogers, Middleton, check the registration desk. See if you find anyone."

Two firefighters rushed inside. Daria tapped her foot.

She expected them to escort Shelby out at any moment. Instead, next to her, the radio clipped to the firefighter's shoulder crackled to life. "Lieutenant, you need to see this."

"Stay here." He left her standing in the freezing parking lot and ran inside.

Tears threatened her police composure. "Please be okay." Daria bit her lip and waited for their return. She glanced back and spotted Jake motioning for her. He held a serious look, with his lips drawn tight, and sat with that staunch marine posture. Her gaze returned to the hotel entrance before she met him at the car's passenger window. She placed her hand on the edge of the glass.

"What's going on?" Jake rested his hand on hers, and the gentleness of his touch sent warmth through her. She stepped out of his reach and sensed him eyeing her. He pulled his hand back inside the car. "You were right about the weather. I would come help, but I've got a tiny bundle in the back and I can't leave her alone."

"No worries. I've got this. You're doing the right thing protecting her." Daria lowered her eyebrows at him. "They're checking to see if they can find Shelby."

"Is she related to you?"

"No. She's single, working her way through nursing school. I've helped her out a few times since her parents died in a boating accident several years back."

"That's humanitarian of you." Jake broke eye contact with her. "I think I see movement inside."

Daria pointed to Jake's car. "Stay with Emma. I'll let you know what happens."

His body language said he wanted to be among the

action. But he'd confirmed taking care of a baby was his priority. She returned to the middle of the parking lot and waited for the firefighters to exit.

She glanced back at Lieutenant Jeffers, who approached and stood by her. "What's the update?" He rubbed his hands together in the cold.

Daria explained about her friend working at the front desk. The lieutenant had given her a hard time for months since she'd messed up and lost her temper a while back. Now that she'd completed anger management classes and had an important case, she wished he'd show her more respect. She'd done as he asked.

He coughed and spat on the frozen ground. "Remember to maintain a professional relationship with your victim. Any signs otherwise, and I'll pull you from the case."

She bit her lip. Just because she knew Jake from their school days didn't automatically put them in a relationship. She was only there to protect him and his niece from whoever had targeted them. Who knew she'd be involved in a murder case and be assigned to watch over the two of them? If she solved the crime, it could give her a chance to prove herself with her fellow officers and make her lieutenant proud.

The hotel doors pushed open, and two firefighters carried someone out. A lump formed in her throat. *Please don't let her be dead.*

Paramedics met the firefighters just outside the door with a gurney.

Daria rushed over. "Is she okay?"

Shelby's hand reached out to her. Daria took her hand

and looked down at the badly bruised face of her friend. "Shelby, who did this to you?"

One of the medics stepped in the way, causing her to drop Shelby's hand. "You can question her once we check her out. She's received several blows to the face, and she has a large hematoma on the back of her head."

"Did you fall and hit your head?" the other paramedic asked.

"No." A whisper slipped from Shelby's lips.

"We're going to transport you to the hospital."

Daria slipped around the paramedic. "Just give me a minute." She turned to Shelby. "Can you talk? What happened?"

"A man came into the hotel right before you did, asking for an area map. We usually have them available for tourists." Shelby winced and reached for her bruised forehead. "When I turned back around, he punched me in the eye. That's why I had my sunglasses on. He hid in my office with a gun. But once you'd checked in and left, he returned and used my face as a punching bag and I must have passed out. He threatened my life if I mentioned he'd been there. He knew you were bringing someone to the hotel, and forced me to give him a specific room number. He took my master key."

Heat rose to Daria's cheeks. How did he know they were coming to the hotel? Daria maintained control of her anger. She smoothed her finger across Shelby's hand. "These paramedics will take care of you. Can you describe the man who assaulted you?"

"Not really. With the drop in temperatures, it was understandable that he'd wear a sock cap and a bulky black coat. I won't forget his beady green eyes, though."

Daria's skin crawled. She'd just described the attire of the man who stood in the shadows at the corner of the hotel, except she hadn't seen his eyes. Guilt gripped her for the second time. It was all her fault. She'd put Jake and Emma in danger, and now Shelby. How could she prove herself a good cop if she kept messing up?

"We need to get her to the hospital," the paramedic said. He and his partner rolled the gurney to the ambulance.

"I'll check on you later." Daria walked over and updated her lieutenant and coworkers before joining Jake and Emma in the car.

"Is she okay?" Jake adjusted the heat vent.

"Yes. I think so. Someone punched her in the face and hit her over the head. They're taking her to the hospital. Have you spotted anyone acting suspicious?"

Daria placed her gloved hands on the steering wheel and studied all the activity going on in the parking lot. The ambulance drove away, and firefighters sprayed water that froze as drops landed on the pavement. Police officers taped off the entrance to the parking lot and blocked bundled-up passersby as they crowded around to watch the action. Who would want to stand in the snowy, freezing temperatures at two fifteen in the morning? Was the person responsible for the fire among them, fuming over his failure to eliminate Jake and Emma?

"Not yet, but that doesn't mean—"

Daria jumped from the car and took off running toward the crowd. Her feet skidded on the slick parking lot. She managed to stay upright. The hooded figure she'd seen earlier at the corner of the hotel stood at the back of the crowd.

He bolted, ran across the street and down an alley that split and led behind the town's businesses. She pushed through the crowd. He disappeared before she could continue the chase.

She radioed her fellow officers. Several arrived and began searching the back doors of businesses and parked cars. A light snow carpeted the alley. His foot-prints disappeared in a freezing pool of water leaking from a faucet. It was useless to track him in the dark with the frigid weather. She must get Jake and Emma to a safe place.

Daria made her way back to the car. She pulled her gloves off and held her hands over the heat vents. "I missed him."

"Missed who? What happened?" He faced her.

"I spotted the guy who'd been standing at the corner of the hotel. I lost him, though."

Jake opened his car door and stepped out. "Tell me where you last saw him, and I'll track him."

"No. You're staying put." She sensed tension rising.

He got back in the car and shut the door. His nar-rowed eyes confirmed his frustration. She touched his arm. "I'm here to protect you and Emma. Whoever set up that explosion knew what they were doing to target your specific room. The fire chief will do his investi-gation and let us know."

Emma threw her cup on the floor. "Bite." She reached her hand out and wiggled her fingers. "Bite."

"When was the last time you fed her?" Daria reached for the diaper bag. "Aren't there snacks in here?"

"I gave her juice and some of those puffy cheese sticks." Jake helped remove items from the bag. "I'll see if there's something else I can give her."

"I'm talking about an actual meal. And have you changed her diaper?" Daria eyed Jake.

Jake wiped his face with his hand. "I changed her before she went to bed. That's why she has her pajamas on. The attempted abduction and the shooting earlier messed with our routine. I've only given her snacks. She's a good baby. But in answer to your question, no she hasn't had a, quote, unquote, proper meal since breakfast. I'm surprised she hasn't screamed."

"Babies require a meal just like we do. We get hungry, Emma gets hungry, and sometimes more often. They enjoy snacks, but a healthy meal is better and lasts longer."

"I get it." He located the cheese puffs and handed Emma one. "Where can we get something to eat at three in the morning?"

Daria buckled her seat belt. "I know just the place. Buckle up." She pulled up close to Jeffers for permission to leave the scene. He waved her on.

She exited the parking lot, thankful for minimal traffic on the slick street. In about three more hours, the town would come alive with more vacationers, where accidents were likely to happen.

Jake turned back around, facing the front of the vehicle, and propped his elbow on the edge of the car's window. "In the war, we went long hours before stopping to eat or drink. I've got to think about Emma's needs above my own."

"You'll get used to it. She will let you know when

she's hungry. Just like now. Besides, you know you can trust me. I'm here for you." She bit her lip. Investigating Jake's case could make or break her career, and dissolve or resolve a new friendship with him. A man she'd always cared about.

I need Your wisdom, Lord.

Her cell rang. Why was Officer Cramer calling her this late? She opted not to put it on speaker.

"Officer Gordon here."

"Daria, I received a call from an anonymous lady who insisted on having a confidential meeting with you," Cramer said.

"Kind of late or early to be getting calls, isn't it?" Daria's inquisitive radar went up. "Could be a setup. When did she want to meet?"

"Right away." Cramer's words fell flat. "Said this couldn't wait. She'll meet you at the twenty-four-hour café."

Daria didn't have to guess which café. The town only had one that stayed open all night.

"Did she say what was so important that it required an immediate meeting at this time of the morning?" Daria hadn't wanted to encounter anyone else tonight, but if it helped the case, she'd take a moment.

Cramer cleared his throat. "Only that it was a matter of life or death."

"What was that all about?" Jake evaluated Daria's body language. Something had shifted her thoughts. Her eyebrows lowered, and she'd pursed her lips.

Her eyes cut toward him as though she debated answering his question. "A woman wants to meet me at the restaurant."

"This late? Someone you know?" He looked out of the rear window to see if someone was following them. Not a vehicle in sight, only their tire marks in the light snow. "What about? If you don't mind me asking?"

"Didn't say other than it's a life-or-death situation." Daria slid her hands around the steering wheel of Jake's car, then gripped it again at the three and nine position. Her knuckles whitened slightly with her grip.

"Is it about our case?" A renewed burst of energy rushed over him at the thought of more evidence that could help solve the murder of his sister and brother-in-law.

"Our case? Jake, this investigation is in the hands of the department. There's no 'ours' about it. You need to focus on Emma and let us do our job."

Jake swallowed his pride. Well, partly. He'd still like to get his hands on the person responsible for almost killing an innocent baby. He valued his own life, but he'd give it for Emma's safety, or Daria's. Part of that safety was caring for Emma's needs. After all, she was a little human who had the same basic needs he did. Only in smaller portions. Something he'd have to keep in mind.

Daria held firm to her status as a police officer, and he admired her tenacity despite his constantly over-stepping the boundaries. Everything inside him wanted to go into stealth mode and seek the enemy. He could sneak around better alone, but what would he do with Emma? There was another dilemma he'd have to fig-ure out. Was Emma supposed to go with him everywhere now? Could he handle someone tied to his side for the rest of his life? He rubbed his forehead. What was he thinking? Yes, he could and would adapt to having Emma in his life forever.

"I assume we are going to meet this anonymous person right now?" He handed Emma another cheese puff. "Come to think of it, I haven't eaten, either. Just hasn't been a priority." He rested his arm on the passenger door's armrest.

"I know it's late, but we all have to eat." Daria kept her eyes on the road as she drove and talked. "It's like adding fuel to the car. Food adds strength to our bodies. But you already knew that."

Jake weighed Daria's comment. Of course, he knew the necessity of keeping the body nourished. His thoughts flashed back to active duty, hiding in the bunker with everyone ready for battle, and how he reminded everyone to drink plenty of water and eat, to stay alert and watch for the enemy.

"Yeah, I'm aware of keeping the body fueled." His tone came out a little sharper than he'd intended. Plans for his future took a U-turn in a moment's time with one phone call announcing his sister's death and then becoming a substitute dad. Uh, and mom. So much for becoming a career marine. To be so smart and concerned for the safety of his men, he now had to turn that focus on the needs of his niece. He must pull himself together and focus better.

Daria's silence had him wondering if he'd upset her. He had to stifle his need to be in control and work alongside her. They were great friends years ago. Could they slide back into that same status now, or possibly shift to dating and see where it would lead? Her shoulder-length brown hair complemented her unblemished complexion, and her uniform only enhanced her good looks. She was intelligent, determined and protective. And she loved babies. Traits he appreciated.

She slammed on the brakes. "Look out."

He grabbed the dash with one hand and stretched his other arm out toward Emma, mere seconds before a car ran a stop sign. It slid on the icy street, turned around, then headed straight toward them. Daria pressed the accelerator, but the tires spun. She inched forward and slowly picked up speed, but not fast enough.

They were going to crash.

Jake dove over the front seat and covered Emma with his body. His long legs landed on the dash and kicked the ceiling of the car. A hard hit shoved his car sideways and through the intersection. Emma let out a scream. Her deep brown eyes widened, and her lower lip quivered. He kissed her forehead, smoothed her curls and quickly grabbed the other sippy cup that had fallen out of the diaper bag.

Emma took the cup with one hand and patted Jake's cheek with the other. She put the cup to her lips.

"It's okay. Uncle Jake won't let anything happen to you." One hard shove and he was back in the front seat. "Daria, are you hurt? Did you get a good look at the driver? He clipped the back fender and sped away." He placed his hand on her shoulder.

She clipped her dangling police radio mic back on her shoulder. "I'm fine, just furious I couldn't maintain better control. How about you and Emma?"

"We're good, but if my car is still drivable, we might

need to get moving before he returns and rams us again."
Jake buckled himself in while Daria reported the incident.

"We can't leave the scene, Jake. There might be evidence on the road that will direct us to whoever did this." She opened the driver's door. "And, no, I didn't get a good look at the driver. The tinted windows made sure of that."

A blast of frigid air swept through the car as she stepped out. Sirens blared from the distance. Jake opened his passenger door and eased from the front seat, then opened the back door. He wrapped the blanket snugly around Emma and scooped her into his arms. Sleet mixed with snow hit his face. He made sure the blanket covered Emma's head.

Daria turned in circles, studying the area. She turned to Jake and patted Emma on the back. "Why don't you take her over to that store's covered awning and get her out of the snow? Hold her close. It will help keep her warm. It's not safe to stay in the street by the car right now."

"What about you?" Jake wasn't used to leaving a lady alone in a dangerous situation, and it didn't feel right even if she was a cop.

"I'll stay here and explain what happened. Now, go. Take care of Emma." Her words held authority and concern. "When a squad car arrives, the two of you can get in the back so you can stay warm."

Jake did as he was told. He made it under the awning and stepped close to the store's door to avoid the wind. He readjusted his hold on Emma. She bent her knees and scrunched in the blanket. She was cold. His heart went out to this small bundle. He shivered too. The squad car couldn't get there fast enough.

Daria, the scrawny little girl he used to know, stood tall in the middle of the street, with her hands at her waist. She was still turning in circles keeping watch. He reveled in the difference a few years had made in her. She could be on his team any day with her tough yet sensitive and fearless demeanor.

Three police cars with sirens blaring and lights flashing pulled onto the scene. Emma's head swung around. She pulled her arm out of the blanket and pointed.

"See." She looked him in the eyes. A couple of tears slipped down her cheeks.

"I see. Do you like the flashing lights?" He wiped her tears, patted her back and tried to cover her.

Daria motioned them to the squad car. He didn't hesitate. With ice steadily forming on the road, he'd have to be sure-footed. He recognized two of the officers as Cramer and McDaniel. They walked over and joined another officer while Daria met him at the car and held the back door open for them. Jake wasn't used to anyone holding the door for him or trying to take care of him. Kind of nice. The warm car thawed his almost frozen fingers. He'd never complain about how cold he was, though. He was a marine.

The quiet of the night suddenly came to life. A car with a loud motor slid around the corner of the intersection and started shooting as it sped away. The officers fired back. Daria dove into the back across Jake's legs, covering them with her body.

McDaniel rushed back to them. Cramer and the other officer hopped in their cars and chased after the speeding vehicle. Daria pushed against the floorboard to get out. Jake placed Emma in the seat and helped Daria get up. For a moment, they were face-to-face, staring into each other's eyes. Amid the danger, he had an overwhelming urge to kiss her, which caught him off guard.

FIVE

Daria stretched her arm out of the car to Officer Mc-Daniel, who took her hand and pulled her to her feet. She dared not look back at Jake. What had just happened? Was he still looking at her? His expressive eyes pierced hers in a way she'd never experienced. Kind of like…he wanted to kiss her. She scolded herself for thinking that way. Certainly she'd misread him. It wasn't the time, nor the place, to entertain personal thoughts. Besides, Lieutenant Jeffers wouldn't approve.

"Looks like they shot randomly into the air." McDaniel shook his head. "Good way to get yourself killed."

"A warning, you suppose? The whole incident looks suspicious." She pushed the fallen strands of hair back behind her ears. "I'm glad no one was hurt."

"Where were you going at this hour?" McDaniel shoved his hands into his pockets.

"The twenty-four-hour restaurant. We haven't had dinner. It's about breakfast time now." A shiver crawled over her body. "That's the vehicle his deceased sister left him. I need to get the baby's car seat."

"I'll get it. You stay with Jake and Emma." McDaniel walked toward Jake's vehicle in time to meet with the approaching wrecker.

The driver hopped out of his truck and rubbed his hands together, then got to work loading the SUV. By the time he finished, the sleet and snow had stopped. Temperatures still hung in the twenties with frigid gusts of wind.

She turned and stared at the squad car where Jake and Emma were, out of the cold. She could tell Jake itched to help, but he continued showing his love for Emma by staying with her and protecting her. He might be a tough marine, but he had a heart of compassion.

She returned to the squad car and found Emma sleeping soundly, holding her cup in one hand and her little bunny in the other. She looked content and comfortable. A sigh slipped from her lips.

A hand gripped her arm through the car window. She spun.

"Are you okay?" Jake squeezed her arm.

"I'm thankful no one was hurt. Yes, I'm okay. Please stay here while I assist McDaniel so we can get out of here." Daria picked up a couple of car parts she could handle and dropped them together at the curb. Icicles had formed on the cold metal and sparkled with the reflection of the only streetlight around the area.

Cramer and the other officer returned to the scene and helped the wrecker finish clearing debris from the street.

"I'll drive you back to the station where you can file your report and get one of the impounded cars off the back lot." McDaniel said. "We're not allowed to ride civilians around in police cruisers unless it's a special case. I suppose this one qualifies as special."

"Thanks." *So much for meeting with the anonymous person.* They may have missed out on meeting the lady. If it was that important, maybe she'd call again. Her stomach told her they still needed to eat. A hot meal would be nice.

The station was a welcomed sight and a warm place to file her report. She grabbed her iPad and showed Jake where to get them a cup of coffee. They returned to the same conference room they'd been in earlier. Daria had placed the couch cushion on the floor and put a table-cloth from the credenza over it. Jake placed sleeping Emma on the cushion, took her coat off and covered her with her blanket.

Daria sat at the table and began her report. In a few minutes, Jake returned with two cups of steaming caffeine. He set one in front of her and moved to the opposite side of the table with his cup. Her report took longer than normal because of all the details she had to remember. Jake tapped the table. She sensed him staring at her.

"Why aren't you married by now?" Jake's inquisitive look and off-the-wall question took her by surprise.

She leaned back in her chair and twisted the stylus between her fingers. "I thought I answered your question earlier. I'm busy with my job, and no one around here is my type."

Jake's eyebrows lifted and a smirky grin rolled across his face. "What exactly is your type?"

Wish he wouldn't do that. He is already handsome enough.

She grinned. "Well, I suppose a tall, broad-shouldered, burly, strong and intelligent man that resembles a marine, maybe."

He pointed to himself. "Are you calling me burly?" He flexed his biceps.

"Who said I was talking about you?" Her insides warmed. At first, she was joking, but it hit her that having him around all the time wasn't a bad thought.

"Oh, pardon me. I can tell there's a line of marines at the door waiting for your approval." The sparkle in his eyes lightened the moment.

"They must call for an appointment to meet with me. It's imperative I interview them before making a decision." She burst out laughing. "You are impossible. Let me go get that car. We still need to eat and feed the little darling."

His stomach growled. He slapped his hand over his belly. "Guess that says it all. Let's go."

She paused at the door and pointed to the drawn curtains. "In case you haven't noticed, the sun's coming up. It's actually time for breakfast."

Daria closed the door behind her and pulled on her police-issued coat. The back lot had a few icy places, but for the most part it was clear. Maybe the town's streets would be in the same condition or clearer.

A black midsized car lit up when she clicked the key fob. She unlocked it and got inside. The cold leather sent chills down her legs.

Brrr. Warm this thing up.

The motor started on cue. She pulled around to the back door and put Emma's car seat in the back. Jake stepped out with Emma and buckled her in.

Emma whined and stretched out her arm, opening and closing her hand. "Bunny. Bunny."

"Where's her little rabbit, Jake? Check in the conference room."

In a matter of seconds, Jake returned and handed her the small rubber bunny. She settled back and leaned her head against the car seat's headrest, bouncing the white rabbit on her leg. "It was in the hallway. She'd dropped it."

"It's strange how children get so attached to things. Usually, it's a blanket or stuffed animal, but a small rubber rabbit?" Daria pulled into the early morning traffic. A few cars were on the street and a couple of people wrapped up in coats walked along the sidewalk.

"You've got me. I've been overseas on active duty." He pulled the visor down. "That sun's bright. Anyway, I guess Amanda bought them for her. There's a complete set of little rubber animals in the bottom of her diaper bag. A kid thing, I suppose."

Daria turned into the parking lot of the twenty-four-hour restaurant and parked. The red Open Twenty-Four Hours sign blinked like lights on a Christmas tree against the window. Visitors couldn't miss the building with its yellow painted wood structure. "I suppose my mystery person gave up a long time ago. If it's important, she'll reschedule."

"I hope she's still here. I'm curious about what she wants," Jake said. "I can smell bacon frying." He unbuckled Emma and pulled her out. "Do you smell bacon, Emma? It's delicious. You might have to try it." He kissed her cheek.

They reached the restaurant's clear glass door. Daria opened it for him.

"No, I've got the door. You go," Jake said.

"Just go." Daria nodded.

"Nope. Ladies first." He held the door open as they had a standoff.

"Fine." She went inside first. The sign read Seat Yourself. "Any preferences?"

"Booth in the back, by the emergency exit door. I like to see what's going on." He walked that way.

Daria stopped off and picked up a high chair. She recognized the senior man sitting on a stool at the breakfast bar. "Mr. Treadway, you're up early. Are you still staying busy at the Oakland Grill?"

"Busier than I'd like, but it keeps me going." He took a drink of his coffee and set it down as he turned and looked at her. "Well, I do say you are out mighty early, too. I see you have company." He smiled and winked.

"Yep, something like that. You enjoy your coffee and stay warm."

"Hey, I need to talk to you." He pointed to Daria.

"Can it wait? I'm pretty busy right now." Daria patted him on the back.

"Sure, sure. I don't want to interfere." He nodded.

Daria returned to their table and placed the high chair at the end. Jake sat Emma down and scooted the chair closer. She rubbed her eyes, then pounded the bunny on the table.

"That was Mr. Treadway. He refuses to retire, so he helps at a restaurant in the middle of town. He said he wanted to talk to me."

"About what?" Jake caught Emma's toy before it fell off the table. "Working will keep him young."

"Bite, phees." Her hand opened and closed. "Mama, bye-bye." She kicked her legs. "Bite. Bite."

A gray-haired server carrying a tray approached their table with two coffees and a child's cup of apple juice and fries. "Here you go. You two looked like you need a kick start this morning, and this little doll has been here before. Her mom always ordered her apple juice and french fries." She placed a small box of dry cereal in front of Daria. "Her mom always packed one of these in the side pocket of her diaper bag. Thought you might want an extra."

"Thank you," Jake said. "Good to know." He unzipped the empty pocket and stuffed it inside.

Emma dropped the rabbit and clutched the cup with both hands, then put one hand down and picked up a fry.

Daria lifted her eyebrows. "You knew her mother?"

The server threw her hand in the air joyfully. "My, yes. Amanda was in here every week, like clockwork. She and Emma always sat at the table by the window. She and Tom came in here without Emma the morning of their tragic accident."

"Do you know of anyone who was upset with Amanda?" Daria hoped the server had more information.

"Heavens, no. Everyone loved her and her husband." The server pulled out her order pad. "What would you like to eat this morning?"

They placed their order and sipped on the hot coffee. A woman on the opposite side of the restaurant wearing sunglasses and a scarf wrapped around her head and across her nose and face moved from one table to another until she was close to where they sat. Daria tensed and patted her side where she'd holstered her weapon. Could this be the woman who wanted to meet with her?

"I'll be back in a minute." Daria slipped from the booth and approached the woman. "Did you make an appointment to meet someone?"

"Yes." She looked around nervously. "I've been waiting all night."

"Who did you have an appointment with?" It didn't hurt to double-check.

."You." She ducked her head and looked·up again.

Daria sat down and waited for the lady's explanation. She spotted Mr. Treadway leaving the restaurant. She'd find him later.

"The baby over there is Emma, right? That's Amanda and Tom's daughter. Am I correct?" She bit her lip.

"First, what's your name and your connection with this family?" Daria sized the lady up. She looked nervous and even frightened.

"I'm Liz Colton. I worked at the bank with Amanda. I'd seen pictures of her baby on her desk, then after the accident, I saw the child's picture with her parents in the paper."

"Ms. Colton—Liz. Why did you want to meet with me, and why don't you take those sunglasses off and uncover your face so I can see you?"

"Can't do that. Someone might recognize me. I had to tell you I believe they murdered Amanda because she discovered something illegal going on at the bank and downloaded documents on toy flash drives."

Chills raced down Daria's spine, and it wasn't the cold air. "Toy flash drives?"

"Yes." Liz pointed at Emma playing with the bunny. "You might check what she has in her hand."

Seriously?

Was it possible the little bunny Emma held on to so tightly held incriminating evidence? She could hardly hold herself in her seat, but she had to hear Liz out.

"What else can you tell me?" Daria tried not to sound aggressive with her questioning. Finally, some concrete evidence, maybe.

"Our manager came in and didn't shut his door all the way. I overheard him talking on the phone. No idea who he was talking to, but he stated his hidden camera caught Amanda downloading private files that could cause his empire to crumble. He said if that flash drive landed in the wrong hands, it might implicate him and upper management in embezzlement. If they could crack the codes. Then he laughed."

"What did Amanda do when she realized they suspected her?"

"She fought tears and wondered what they'd do to her. She started receiving death threats if she didn't return the private documents. Amanda was a go-getter. She'd gone this far, so she had to have the rest of the files. I told her to go to the police. She went to the station and filed a report, but they didn't take her seriously. Her last words to me were if anything happened to her, to make sure her family knew how much Emma loved her little rubber toys. Amanda told me to find you and tell you what happened." Liz picked up her purse and pushed it up on her shoulder.

"Why me? Can you come down to the station and give your statement?" Daria scooted to the edge of her seat. Liz was about to bolt. "How can I get in touch with you?"

"She knew you from childhood and trusted you. I've stayed too long. Don't try to contact me. They'll kill me, too, if they find out I know stuff. I'm sorry for Jake's loss, but I've got to go." She stood, straightened her coat and rushed out into the cold.

Jake tapped his foot on the tile floor. What was going on between that lady and Daria? He scooted to the edge of the red fake leather seat with intentions of finding out, but the woman darted outside. Daria returned to the table.

"What happened? Fear was in that woman's eyes." Jake leaned in toward Daria and lowered his voice. "What did she say? Was it about Amanda?"

"Yes." Daria blew out a breath. "But let's check on something first." She picked up the little rubber bunny that Emma had let go of to eat her fries. "Watch this." She pulled the top from the bottom and a flash drive appeared.

Jake sucked in a breath. "Is it real?"

"As real as they come, just in novelty form. Who would suspect something that looks like a child's toy?" Daria snapped the two pieces back together and placed it back on Emma's tray.

Jake reached into the diaper bag and pulled out the collection of rubber toys. Daria and he pulled apart each little farm animal, and sure enough, they were all flash drives. He dropped his hands on the table. "I cannot believe we've had the evidence with us all along. What did she tell you?"

Daria explained what Liz had to say. She had confirmed his suspicions that his sister's death wasn't an accident. She'd been murdered. They put the toys back together and tucked them into the firm bottom of the diaper bag, where Amanda had hid them.

"Finish eating. We've got work to do." Daria bit into her breakfast sandwich and stuffed a tater tot into her mouth. "We need our energy."

Normally he could down a big cheeseburger in two bites, but Daria's news stole his appetite. She was right. They needed food for strength. He conceded and did his best to shove down some of his breakfast.

Emma hummed and mashed french fries on the high chair tray as she ate. It was a relief to see her satisfied and playful. Oh, how Amanda and Tom must have adored her. He did, too. His heart broke all over again for his loss. He sucked it up and pulled himself together. Like Daria said, they had work to do.

As soon as they finished eating, they walked toward their vehicle. Clouds had moved in, and large snowflakes hit him in the face. The brisk wind whipped around his ears and sent a shiver across his shoulders. Emma's little eyes blinked fast as snow landed on her nose.

"It's cold out here, Emma. Do you like the snow?" He patted her back and wrapped the blanket tighter. She pushed her arm out into the cold air and slapped at the fluffy flakes.

He paused and squinted at what appeared to be writing on the back of their car. The words were almost covered with snow. He deciphered *Hot Head*, evidently written with shaving cream. He shot a glance at Daria.

Her face turned as red as the flashing Open sign in the restaurant's window.

"Is this some kind of joke? Was it intended for you?" He put Emma in the car seat and stepped back.

"It's nothing. Let's go." Daria hopped in the car and turned on the windshield wipers, pushing the newly fallen snow to small piles at the sides of the glass.

Officer McDaniel pulled in beside their vehicle, studied the almost hidden white writing fading quick, and rolled his window down. He chuckled. "Some of the guys are hazing you. Don't pay any attention to it. A quick wash at the drive-through will erase it or it could freeze in these temperatures." He rolled his window up and got out. "Have a good one. I'm going for my coffee and gravy and biscuits."

McDaniel walked away. Jake placed his hand on Daria's shoulder.

"Is there a story behind this hazing thing?" He spoke as softly as he could. Obviously, the message hurt her feelings. If someone was willing to do that, who knew what else they might do.

"Yes. It's embarrassing and partially true." She propped her arms across the steering wheel. "Last year, we had a lot of tourists. Most of them were pleasant and enjoyed themselves. There was one guy and his dad who'd had too much to drink. The son became a menace to others. His disrespectful behavior, name-calling and aggression grew worse. He refused to settle down after I warned him several times. I lost my temper and arrested him for disturbing the peace. Now some of my coworkers think I have a short fuse and I don't have what it takes to be a cop. I plan to prove them wrong."

Jake rubbed his hands together, then wiped one hand down his face. Harassment was wrong. He didn't appreciate the judgment passed on her and their public display of humiliation.

"Who are these guys?" Names would help him confront the right people.

"I'll not disclose their names. I have my suspicions about who instigated the whole thing." She sat back and started the car. "Let's get to the station and see what's on Emma's drives."

Snow packed fast on her windshield and the wipers fought to clear the glass. Her phone rang. She answered and put it on speaker.

"Officer Daria Gordon."

"Daria, this is Allan Simmons, Kimbleton's fire marshal. The report came back on the hotel fire. It's been confirmed the fire started after someone placed two bug bombs on the mantel of the gas fireplace. Once the fumes built up and reached the pilot light, it exploded. I'm glad Jake ran when he did, or this wouldn't have ended well."

"So it wasn't a bomb." Daria's eyebrows lowered. "Please let me know if anything else comes up."

"Yes, ma'am. Give me a call if you have any more questions."

"Thank you for the update." She disconnected the call. Her eyes met with Jake's. "You were right. The perpetrator purposely planned your demise. Emma's too."

He and Emma were the targets. Not that he needed any more confirmation. Someone had already proven Emma and he were in their crosshairs. His fingernails dug into his palms the tighter he squeezed his fists. The stakes were high and deadly.

He looked over his shoulder at Emma. Her head rested against the side of the car seat, and she held the little rubber bunny up against her neck as her eyes had grown heavy. She'd be asleep soon. He couldn't let anything happen to her.

The windshield fogged up. Daria turned the defroster on high.

Jake retrieved a cloth bib from Emma's diaper bag and wiped the inside of the windshield. Heat from the defroster cleared their view and began melting most of the flakes. Last night's light dusting had turned into a heavy snowstorm. He shifted his eyes to the almost covered side mirror. A dark green truck followed close behind them.

"That truck has been behind us for a while now." He turned and looked out of the rear window. Lines from the rear defrost slowly melted the ice, but still hindered his view.

"It pulled in behind us as soon as we left the restaurant. Why?"

"Looks like we're being followed." He stared at Daria before looking in the side mirror again. His pulse gained speed.

"It's not a tail, if that's what you're thinking." Daria's eyes sparkled and her lips smoothed upward. His stomach flipped. That was the look she gave him multiple times when they were younger. Best friends forever, they'd say, until he'd moved away and lost touch.

She continued, "It's a plainclothes cop escorting us

to the station. I should have told you he'd be following us. Relax. You're jumpy."

"No, I'm not." He straightened. "I'm alert and cautious."

"Is that so?" She laughed. "Then how come it took you five minutes to notice?"

"I spotted it right off but was keeping an eye on it. Besides, Emma distracted me for a minute." He grinned, finding humor in his poor excuse.

"Ohhh, so now you're going to blame a defenseless child."

"You still laugh the same." He put his hand on her shoulder and grew serious. "I've missed that sound." An old memory popped into his head of them, running and jumping in a pile of leaves as kids, then rolling down the hill, laughing until their stomachs hurt. He was too grown up now to do such childish things. Maybe Emma would enjoy the fun when she got older.

Daria's expression grew serious. He hadn't meant to kill the joking between them.

"I often wondered what happened to you. I even watched football for several years, expecting the announcer to scream 'and there goes Jake Fisher, quarterback for the Eagles executing a perfect throw.'" She slowed and turned the corner. "It's nice to see you again."

"Yes, it's great to reconnect. Having a trustworthy friend in town makes life a little easier." He'd purposely shut down any discussion about relationships or dating. Not that he was totally against it; he just didn't think he was ready now that he had Emma. That was a lot to swallow.

Jake checked his side mirror again and noted smoke inside the cab of the green truck. The cop's vision had been obscured and he swerved and stopped. "The inside of our escort's truck is smoking. He isn't behind us anymore."

"What do you mean? Is it on fire?" He noted her eyes went to the rearview mirror.

Jake tensed. "No. Something isn't right. I can feel it."

Daria called the station and reported the green truck might be on fire. "We're almost there, Jake. Hang on. Maybe they can tell us what's happening."

Crash!

Emma screamed.

Someone rammed them. In broad daylight. Their car thrust forward.

"Where did that come from?" Daria worked the steering wheel and kept them on the slick road. "Who knew we're driving this car?"

"It's a black truck. It's coming at us fast." Jake reached back and pressed the blanket to Emma's chest. Somehow, he needed to get her out of harm's way. "Watch out. He's about to hit us again."

SIX

Daria gripped the steering wheel tighter. Her pulse went into overdrive. Her protective radar skyrocketed. "Maybe he'll back off when we reach the station. Is it the same black vehicle you spotted through the forest after the shooting at your house?"

"Could be, but I can't make a positive ID," Jake said.

She pressed the accelerator to go faster than she preferred in the winter conditions, with two civilians in the car. There was nothing she could do. The station was within view. She radioed for help moments before she had to turn.

Wham!

The truck shoved her vehicle past the station's driveway. Daria slid sideways, then straightened. "He's got nerve chasing us right here. I have no choice but to keep going. Maybe I can lose him on Chisel Road."

"Want you," Emma cried out.

"Give her the cup, Jake, and pray that settles her for a bit." Daria bit her lip. She'd asked Jake to pray, as if she thought it would help. Maybe it would. "We can't take her out of the car seat."

Jake reached into the back and handed her the cup. Daria glanced in the rearview mirror. Emma sniffled as she drank.

"Isn't Chisel Road that winding road where we used to get carsick?" Jake eyed Emma, concerned for her safety. "In this weather, I'm not sure I'd risk it. Why not circle back toward the station?"

"Can you get a make on the truck?" Heat rushed to Daria's face. She had to change the subject.

Why did he keep questioning her decisions as a police officer? She never left town like he had. She knew these roads well and understood it wasn't the best choice, but it might deter the tail and cause him to retreat.

"Looks like an old Durango. I haven't seen one of those in a while."

She made a quick turn onto the curvy road and fishtailed. The truck slid sideways and almost ran off the road. She gained ground, leaving her pursuer behind.

"Whoa." Jake grabbed the dash. "I hope you know what you're doing."

"Stop doubting me." She fumed. "Keep an eye on the truck." Truth was, she now doubted herself. The narrow, snow-covered road made it difficult to keep good traction. Another sharp curve lay ahead. She slowed enough to maintain control.

"Gun," Jake said.

Bullets blew out her back tire the moment she started into the curve.

"Hold on. I can't keep it straight. We're going to crash."

Jake flew into the back seat. The car sailed off the road and banged against trees as it plummeted into a ravine. Air bags deployed, smacking Daria in the face. Emma's screams pierced her ears.

An abrupt halt whipped Daria's neck and slammed her deeper into the air bag. Why hadn't she heard from Jake? Her shoulder hurt and her face stung. She pushed at the air bag and forced her body to turn enough to see Emma. Something covered the child's head.

She reached back as best as she could and tugged at the blanket-wrapped diaper bag Jake must have stuffed in the front of Emma. How had he had the wits or time to do that before the crash? Quick thinking on his part. He probably saved Emma from whiplash or serious injury. He was more of a father figure than he'd given himself credit for.

Jake's legs were across the floor, but she couldn't turn enough to see his face. Emma needed consoling. How could Daria get out of the car?

"Jake." She reached back and touched his leg. "Jake. Answer me. Are you okay?" What kind of question was that when he wasn't moving or speaking?

God, we need Your help.

Icy water rushed over her feet.

"Oh, no, Emma. We're at the edge of the river. I've got to get us out of here."

Daria reached for her radio. Static. Her hands fumbled around the seat until she located her phone wedged between the seat and the console. She punched in 911.

"911. What's your emergency?"

"This is Sergeant Daria Gordon of the Kimbleton Police Department with two civilians in the car. We've been chased down and run off the road at the second curve on Chisel Road. Shots fired. We need backup immediately and medical help."

Her hands shook. She managed to put her phone in her front shirt pocket. Heavy footsteps crunched under the snow and twigs snapped. She sucked in a breath. Whoever was out there was getting closer, and she couldn't reposition her body to see who it was.

Please be here, God. Give me wisdom.

No time to waste. She squeezed through the broken window. Pain shot through her left shoulder. Weakness washed over her. Black dots invaded her eyesight as heat covered her like an electric blanket. She couldn't pass out. Emma and Jake needed her.

Arctic wind hit her face about the same time her feet sank ankle deep in the icy water. Shock from the cold helped pull her from the darkness that tried to consume her. She glanced over the top of the car. Two men had descended into the ravine and were coming toward her with their guns in a ready position.

A surge of energy infiltrated every muscle in her body. She tugged at the back door of the vehicle until it released from the large dent in its side. Metal scraping metal interrupted what silence she'd tried to keep. Jake lay on the floor and wasn't moving. Emma's cries spilled out into the forest for all to hear. She shook Jake. No response. Her heart thrashed against her chest.

Voices grew closer. Those men were about to eliminate them.

"Thought you could get rid of us, didn't you?" a gruff voice said. "You still have something we need."

God, we need Your protection.

This could go one of two ways. She could step from

behind the car with her weapon drawn and face her pursuers, identifying them and hopefully subduing them. Or she could step from behind the car and give them a direct shot to take her out.

Her heart pounded hard. She pressed her lips together, firmed her grip on her Glock and stepped through the water into the open. The two men shot almost simultaneously, followed by two answering shots from close by before Daria had a chance to shoot. One man's gun flew out of his hand. He turned and ran. The other man's shot hit the tree close to Daria's head. He dropped to the ground, yelling. Where did those shots come from? Sirens roared.

Daria spun and spotted Jake hanging out of the broken window on the opposite side of the car, holding his weapon. He nodded and gave her a thumbs-up before he worked his way out of the demolished vehicle with Emma and her blanket in his arms and wrapped her in his coat. He turned a circle before facing her again.

"What is it, Jake?" She spun and searched behind them.

"Checking to see if there's a third shooter hiding out."

"I only saw two." Had she missed something, or was he being extra cautious? She scanned the area. Nothing suspicious. "Did you see more of them?"

"No." He rubbed at his dark, stubby hair. "One can never be too careful. The sounds of the rushing water might make it difficult to hear another shooter lurking nearby."

Sirens grew closer. Blue lights flashed on the road above them. Officers emerged and flooded the area. She'd never been so happy to see blue uniforms against the brilliant sparkling snow. Two officers secured the man shot in the shoulder.

In the distance, three officers walked toward them with the second shooter. The men were read their Miranda rights, then escorted to an ambulance. They'd receive medical treatment before going to jail. Daria could hardly wait to get Jake and Emma settled so she could question the prisoners.

"That was some gutsy move back there. You could have gotten yourself killed." Jake stepped up, holding Emma in one arm. He put the other arm around Daria's shoulders.

"All part of the job. I couldn't let anything happen to you and Emma. If it meant risking my life, then so be it." She ducked away from his arm. Pressure from his hand on her shoulder ached somewhat. Nothing a couple of over-the-counter pain relievers couldn't handle. "Thank you for assisting."

"Instinct." His eyes narrowed. "I'm still uncertain about another shooter out there."

Emma leaned from Jake's hold toward Daria with her arms stretched out. How could these two get to her emotions in such a short time? She loved babies. Even more when they wanted her to hold them. Emma had captured her heart from the beginning.

"Come here, baby. Let's get you warmed up." She took the petite eighteen-month-old and readjusted her blanket. Emma instantly wrapped her arms around Daria's neck, squeezed and laid her head on Daria's sore shoulder. Maybe it was just jammed or strained, and not a torn muscle. At least, she hoped not. The pain wasn't as intense as it had been right after the crash.

Three paramedics came toward them with their back-packs.

"You shouldn't be moving around until we get you checked out." The gray-haired paramedic dropped his gear in the snow and moved toward her.

"Hey, Steve. Glad you guys are here. Check Jake and Emma first." She pointed to Jake. "He was unconscious for a couple of minutes."

"No, I'm good." Jake pointed back at her. "She hit her shoulder and Emma was in her car seat. I shoved the diaper bag in front of her to help cushion the blow. Speaking of diaper bag, I need to get it."

"I got it." One of the firefighters handed it to him. "Fast thinking. You probably saved her from popping her little neck or from whiplash."

"There are enough of us to check all of you." Steve moved toward Daria and Emma. He put the stethoscope to Emma's back while the other paramedics checked Jake. Emma pushed his hands away. "Need to put a pediatric cervical collar around her neck, but she's not going to like it. Little ones rarely do. They'll remove it after a CT scan. Same with you two. These collars are for your protection."

Emma fought with Steve. She pulled at the device, screamed and cried until Jake took her from Daria and walked a distance away from Steve.

"She's been through a lot in the past couple of days." Daria blew her warm breath on her hands. "I pray she doesn't have nightmares."

"Which shoulder hurts?" Steve listened to Daria's heart rate.

"My left shoulder. It's nothing."

Arctic wind stirred the frozen leaves and whisked them around like sleet. "Since everyone is mobile, let's get them out of the cold for triages," Steve said. "We're all freezing, and the baby shouldn't be out in this wind."

"Come on, we're moving to the ambulances," Daria said.

Steve scooped up his gear, as did the other paramedics.

They waited for Jake, Emma and her to move uphill before them. Daria walked beside Jake and Emma. He carried the baby and diaper bag on one side, and she moved to his opposite side. Her foot slipped on the frozen forest floor. Jake's big hand caught her by the left arm up close to her armpit. Intense pain shot through her shoulder.

She screamed and her ears started ringing. Black dots invaded her eyesight, and her knees buckled. Everything went dark.

Two paramedics dropped their gear and caught Daria before she hit the ground. Firefighters from the top of the ravine slid down the hill to help. Jake had the powerful urge to pick her up and carry her, but with a clinging baby in his arms, he couldn't react as fast as he'd wanted.

"Here." Jake held Emma out to one firefighter. She screamed, turned a circle in his arms and grabbed him tight around the neck. "I can carry Daria up to the top."

"No need. A litter is on the way down," the stocky man said. "Besides, that little one needs you right now."

He could carry both. Their weight couldn't compare to the dead weight he'd carried after some of his buddies were wounded or killed in battle. He sensed the need to hold and protect Daria and Emma. Was his hard-core marine status going soft on him already?

"What, what are you doing?" Daria pulled at the belts on the litter. "I'm fine. Let me up."

"They'll let you up once they get you to the top." Jake high-stepped it and caught up with her, holding both arms around Emma. "You passed out."

"Seriously? Well, I'm okay now. I can walk." Daria grimaced.

"I saw that." Jake stared down at her. Her shoulder-length brown hair had fallen from the knot on her head and laced her shoulders. There she was. A more mature Daria. Trustworthy and beautiful. True to her job, willing to sacrifice her life for Emma and him. Such admirable traits in his friend. "You're in pain. Let them check you out. Then we'll be on our way."

Daria's actions reminded him of the story he'd heard from his marine buddy about God. Only God sacrificed His Son's life for everyone in the world. "Trust in Him," his fallen buddy had repeated to the guys in his squad more times than he could count. The realization of Daria's actions stirred his emotions and made him realize the deep truth of his comrade's words. God's Son died for him. Jake swallowed the knot forming in his throat.

One firefighter's foot slipped, causing one end of the litter to tilt sideways. Daria's hand flew into the air. Jake grabbed her hand while the firefighter regained control. Emma curled her arms up against his chest and pulled her knees up. She was cold. He was, too. He let go of Daria's hand and secured his hold on Emma, tucking her blanket snug around her again.

Jake glanced up into the trees and whispered his buddy's brief prayer.

Forgive my hardheadedness, God, and forgive me of my past actions that weren't pleasing to You.

Small snowflakes tapped against his cheeks. The wall of rejection and lack of trust he'd formed after receiving the Dear John letter from his ex-fiancée crumbled the moment his gaze fell on Daria and her willingness to die for him. Even though he'd protected her, too, by disabling the shooters. She was an outstanding cop and a beautiful lady and didn't know it.

His chest swelled. He'd reconnected with his best friend. Could he see her as more than a friend? Better yet, could she see *him* as more than a friend? He chewed the side of his lip.

At the top of the ravine, authorities escorted them to different ambulances. Daria's voice carried over to where Jake sat. "I've got to keep an eye on my victims. They're in danger." He shook his head. She still wanted to protect them, even though she had a hurt shoulder. Eventually, she'd have to come to grips with the fact that he really was a trained marine. His skills were at a different scale than her policing skills. He could take care of himself and keep her and Emma safe.

"You'll go to the hospital and get checked. Same with the others," Jeffers told Daria.

"Yes, sir. What happened to my escort?"

I'd like to know that, too.

"Someone tossed a smoke bomb through his window." Jeffers joined the other officers nearby.

Jake leaned over and looked around the door of the ambulance. Daria lay back on the gurney. She didn't look happy. He sat back and studied his sleepy niece. One of her hands still held on to the neck brace, but her deep breathing showed she was relaxing.

A firefighter approached the ambulance. "We'll get the car out of the ravine and tow it in."

"Thanks, but you might relay that information to Daria." He took the rubber bunny from Emma's grip and replaced it with her cup. She whimpered, but curled her cup against her chest. He dropped the bunny in the diaper bag and pointed to Daria, then paused. "Could you deliver this diaper bag to her, as well? She's in the other ambulance. It's important."

"You've got it." The firefighter strode over to Daria. Jake watched as he handed the bag to her. She looked in his direction, gave him a thumbs-up, then called Lieutenant Jeffers to come back.

Jake could have handed the little rubber toys over, but it was Daria's case. She deserved to do the honors. Her lieutenant's eyebrows lowered as he listened to Daria. Then his eyes widened as she extracted the small rubber animal flash drives and explained the value of them. He motioned for Cramer to bring an evidence bag. Daria dropped the evidence in and dated it according to protocol. Jeffers took the bag to his car and drove away.

Daria's smile said it all. It was her case, as she'd reminded him numerous times, to turn in the suspected evidence that could prove his sister's and brother-in-law's deaths were murder and put the killers behind bars. Jake wouldn't have trusted many people with his sister's case, but Daria was different.

"I need to buckle the child in the car seat. It's built into the captain's chair. You can sit on the bench seat over there and buckle up." The paramedic's voice jolted Jake's attention back to his ambulance. He climbed in, locked the gurney in place and sat beside them while the driver closed the door.

Emma's sleepy eyes opened slightly. She gripped the paramedic's jacket. He took her hands, eased them away and placed them in her lap before buckling her in. Jake settled back and buckled up, keeping his attention on the little figure in the big seat.

The rough ride to the hospital reminded him of riding in a jeep over rocky roads to base camp. Why couldn't the designers of vehicles make them absorb all the bumps for a smoother transfer? Especially for the wounded. Emma succumbed to sleep. Her little head bobbed with each bump in the road.

The ambulance brakes squealed as it came to a stop. They'd arrived at the hospital's emergency entrance. Jake unbuckled Emma, waking her, and stepped out of the vehicle. Once inside, he spotted Daria still lying on a gurney. She insisted she had to guard him and Emma. He couldn't help but smile at her persistence to follow through with her job despite her injury.

She rolled her head sideways and his eyes met with her eyes. She lifted her head from the pillow.

"How is Emma? Are you okay? What did the doctor say?" Daria asked.

"We're fine. We just arrived like you." Jake patted Emma's back. "Let the doc check your shoulder. I'll find you when we're done."

Paramedics wheeled Daria's gurney down the hall to a room. Emma and he followed the nurse to another room, where a cartoon jungle scene decorated the walls.

A small basket of rubber toys in individual packages sat on the counter. Perfect for Emma. Her head popped up off his shoulder. Her eyes widened when she spotted all the bright colors. He admired her uncombed dark curls and how she resembled his sister.

"See." She pointed to the wall with a brightly colored toucan sitting on a brown tree limb with green leaves.

"I see." Jake let her touch the bird on the wall.

A nurse entered and held the basket of toys in front of Emma. "Hello, cutie. Do you want a toy?"

Emma reached over and pulled out a rubber giraffe. A perfect fit for her small hands and a relief to Jake, since she no longer had her little rubber rabbit. He unwrapped it for her. Little girl's giggles and gibberish filled the room and warmed his heart.

After CT scans and a thorough check, the doctor removed their neck braces. He put Emma's coat on her, then he made his way to Daria's room. She sat on the edge of the bed with a sling on her arm and a frustrated look on her face. They'd removed her neck brace, too.

"Knock, knock. Is it okay to come in?" Jake stepped inside at her nod, with his and Emma's discharge papers rolled up like a scroll. "What's the diagnosis?"

Emma pointed at Daria, leaned away from Jake and reached for her with the toy in her hand.

"Oh, you have a new toy. I like your giraffe." She eyed Jake. "Just a bruised muscle." Daria took Emma in her one good arm and kissed her cheek. "The doctor said it would be sore for a few days, but I'll be fine. It won't stop me from doing my job. What about you?"

"Emma had a tiny cut on her arm. They cleaned it

and put a Band-Aid on it. My CT scan went well. I've always been a hardhead." He chuckled.

"That's not funny. We could have all been seriously hurt or killed." Emma squirmed out of Daria's lap. Jake helped her crawl onto the bed and sit up.

A nurse came in with Daria's discharge papers and read her the suggested instructions for healing. "Rest your shoulder as much as possible for forty-eight hours. Use a cold pack every twenty minutes for pain or swelling. If you have any problems, return to the ER."

"I'll make sure she takes it easy," Jake said.

The nurse turned to him with wide eyes.

Oh, no.

She pointed her finger at him. "You need to follow doctor's orders, too, mister. A mild concussion isn't anything to ignore. Marine or not, you've still got to heal." The nurse walked out of the room, leaving the door open.

"What?" Daria's face reddened as she tossed the sling aside and pulled on her coat. "You said you were fine."

"Well, I didn't say those exact words. I just didn't expound on it."

"You are impossible." Her glare had a touch of anger and frustration.

Jake turned his focus on Emma to avoid more eye contact with Daria. Her response had more of an impact on him than he thought it would. Amid her tight lips and glaring eyes, that she cared touched him.

He grabbed the diaper bag he'd spotted on the floor beside the counter and followed Daria to the waiting room, where Jeffers, Cramer and McDaniel sat waiting for them. Her phone beeped. She stopped and pulled out her cell. Jake stood right behind her and couldn't help but see the anonymous message she'd received.

It's not over.

   She looked up at him.
   He turned and scanned the room for anyone who looked suspicious.

SEVEN

Daria shifted her eyes around the hospital's waiting room. Couldn't be one of her coworkers, could it? No. Where was her trust? She searched for movement outside the big hospital window. No one as far as she could see. Maybe someone watched her from the distant thickness of buildings and trees across the street.

She struggled with whether she should tell Jeffers about the text. In one way, she didn't want him to know because he might insist on pulling her off the case or putting Jake, Emma and her in a safe house. However, if she didn't tell, and he found out later, he could suspend her for withholding information, which wouldn't be good for her already shaky record.

She'd faced death with this case too many times already, along with Jake. Emma didn't deserve to be involved. One attack after another and the child still found peace in Jake's arms. Daria paused and closed her eyes for a second.

Lord, thank You for answering my prayer. You spared our lives. Forgive me for not trusting in You and for going my own way. I need You in my life. Every minute of every day. Help me make better decisions that will protect Jake and Emma.

"Are you dizzy or something?" Jake's whisper interrupted her silent prayer. She opened her eyes.

"No. I'm good. Just needed a moment to gather my thoughts and thank the Lord for protecting us." She proceeded across the room toward Jeffers.

He stood as she approached. "Daria, Jake, I'm glad everyone is okay, and especially glad this little one wasn't hurt." He fluffed Emma's curls and shook Jake's hand before facing her. "We've glanced at the flash drives. Every one of them has Excel files loaded with codes instead of names, password-protected charts and money laundering locations. We will need to look deeper into them and see if we can crack the codes. Well done, Daria."

"Wasn't me, sir. Amanda, Jake's sister, risked her life downloading the information." She placed her hand on Jake's arm. "Further investigation should prove her and her husband's crash wasn't an accident. Someone ran them off the road on purpose."

"I commend her for risking everything to stop this crime and bring justice to this city. Thanks to her, we now have evidence to warrant a search." Jeffers pushed his arms through his heavy coat and walked toward the door. "I'm sorry for your loss, Jake."

"Thank you," Jake said.

"Before you go, there's something you need to see." Daria lifted her cell for him to read the threatening message. She could almost read his expression, and it wasn't to her liking.

His eyes narrowed. "I'm placing the three of you in protective custody until we resolve this case."

Daria gasped.

No.

She bit her tongue and calmed herself. "I'd rather you didn't do that. Jake and I are on the verge of busting this case open."

Jeffers straightened his shoulders. "You and Jake? Since when did he join the police department?"

"I didn't mean it like that." She shifted her stance. Wrong choice of words. "I am handling the case according to protocol. And I'd appreciate your allowing me to carry it through."

Jeffers rubbed his chin. His expressive eyes narrowed again. She stood tall with her head held high. Maybe he'd notice she wasn't cowering.

He cleared his throat. "Cramer, you and McDaniel escort the three of them to the safe house."

His comment dropped like a boulder on her confidence. Heat rushed to her cheeks. Jeffers didn't think she could do it, and Jake would witness for himself the distrust of her lieutenant. Embarrassed and humiliated, Daria bit her lip to keep from saying something she shouldn't, which would prove she still had a temper.

Jake stepped forward and was about to speak, but she held her hand up. Thankfully, he backed away. An argument would only make things worse and could cause her to be suspended.

Jeffers's stern gaze turned to her. "Daria, you go with Jake and the baby to the safe house and keep a watch on them. Should a breach take place, they are in your hands."

Adrenaline shot to her toes so fast, she almost jumped up and down. Not an appropriate response for an officer of the law being given an assignment. She held back a relieved smile.

"Yes, sir." Her position, and his belief in her, had been restored, or so she hoped. "Before we go, is it possible for me to question the shooters?"

"Which is it you want, Daria? Bodyguard for the victims or to interrogate the prisoners?" His gruff tone didn't sway her.

"Both, sir." She stood her ground again and glanced at Jake. His slight nod meant he approved.

"Fine. Let's do this." Jeffers let out a huff. "McDaniel, you take them to the station, and Cramer will follow. When she's done, have another seized car ready for her. Then you and McDaniel escort them on to the safe house in unmarked cars."

"You've got it." McDaniel put his coat on, as did Cramer.

Jake pulled the hood of Emma's coat over her head and tightened the blanket around her body. "Now we're talking."

Daria zipped her coat all the way up to her neck. The blustery wind sent chills through to her bones, or so it seemed. Snow covered the ground and made walking a little treacherous. She'd experienced winters like this before and knew the roads would be slick. She paused at the squad car and opened the door.

"Hurry, get Emma out of this wind." Daria placed her hand on Jake's back as he bent and slid into the car.

Another squad car pulled up beside them and the officer jumped out and opened his trunk. What was he doing? He opened their back door and put a child's car seat in. "Roads are too risky to not buckle her in properly," he said.

"Thank you. Remind me to buy you coffee at the doughnut shop sometime." Daria gave the officer a thumbs-up.

"I will. Chocolate glazed is my favorite with black coffee." He backed out of the car. "Drive safe." The door slammed, and he drove away.

"Your lieutenant thought of everything." Jake put Emma in the seat and buckled her in.

"Actually, I knew he had a baby's car seat in his trunk. He always carries one just in case. I sent him a text and asked him to deliver it to us," McDaniel said.

"Good thinking." Daria looked back at a happy Emma playing with her giraffe.

The drive to the station wasn't as bad as she expected. Jake, Emma and she rushed from the squad car into the station. McDaniel drove away. Probably to switch out cars as instructed. The aroma of fresh coffee captured her senses. She turned to Jake, and Emma leaned into Daria's arms. Her shoulder ached, but she'd pop a couple of over-the-counter pain relievers as soon as she put Emma down.

"I smell coffee." Jake darted toward the coffeepot in plain view. "I'll get us some."

"Thanks. I could use a hot cup right now." Daria entered the familiar conference room where Emma and Jake had been before. She set Emma down on the floor and took off her little pink coat. Daria removed her coat, too, and draped it over the back of a chair. Emma's wouldn't hang so she placed it on the table.

Jake entered with their hot beverages. The aroma permeated the room. It smelled so good.

"Here you go." He handed her one and placed sugar and creamer on the table. "I wasn't sure what you wanted in yours. I like mine black. The stronger, the better."

Her hand touched his as she took her coffee. Bigger, stronger hands than she remembered from years earlier. Was her crush from long ago reshaping itself and growing stronger? He must have noticed her pause.

"Your hands are like ice. Hold this cup a minute and you'll warm up." His serious expression didn't match his comment. Had he sensed their connection?

She quickly blew on her hot coffee, took a sip, then walked toward the window. The conference room door opened.

"You ready?" Lieutenant Jeffers stood in the doorway.

"Yes." Daria picked up her pace toward the door. She stopped and looked back. "I might be a while. You and Emma make yourselves at home. You know where the coffee is, and there are snacks in that credenza along the wall. Oh, and be sure to feed Emma that jar of baby food in her diaper bag. She has snacks and juice in there, too."

"Don't worry about us." Jake retrieved Emma's sippy cup from the diaper bag. "I'm learning how to be an uncle."

Daria darted to the front desk where the clerk kept over-the-counter pain meds. She tossed two in her mouth and swallowed them with a sip of her coffee. She rushed down the hallway, down the stairs and into the first interrogation room. After a couple of hours, she'd gathered information, but not everything she needed. Names. She needed names.

Jeffers directed her to move on to the second inter-rogation room where the other shooter waited. By the time she arrived, the guy was more than ready to talk. He and the other man claimed innocence, but that was expected in most any case.

"Tell us who is behind these attacks. Who killed Amanda and her husband?" Daria leaned forward at the table where the shooter sat on the opposite side.

"I had nothing to do with it. Gregory Hall, the bank president, the vice-president and his assistant manager are all involved in money laundering and embezzle-ment. Don't know who put the hit out on that Amanda girl," the man said.

"Why did they want her dead?" Daria sat back and crossed her arms.

He picked at his fingers. Daria slapped the table. He jerked back.

"I asked why they killed her."

"Because she was a threat to their operation. She had to be eliminated. The boss caught her on his hid-den camera, downloading stuff on some type of kid's flash drive. Couldn't let her get away with all that in-formation."

Daria stood and paced the room. "What else can you tell me?"

"I'm a dead man already. They'll kill me if I walk out of here." He straightened in his chair. "I told you who all was involved. I think there's one more person, but I wasn't privy to his name."

Her muscles tightened. Someone still lurked, waiting

for the right opportunity to make his move. Could he or this other person have messaged her from a burner phone? She walked out of the room and leaned against the wall. Jeffers stepped out behind her.

"I'll send officers out to pick up each member of the bank's management team and bring them in for questioning. Murder, mishandling of funds, money laundering and embezzlement. Strong charges if we can get the proof. We need to crack those codes."

She pushed from the wall. "I'll go check on Jake and Emma. I'm sure they're ready to get out of here."

"Head straight for the safe house. You know which one?" Jeffers asked.

"Yes. Four miles outside of town."

"Correct."

The day had flown by with all the trauma they'd encountered, and the questioning took longer than she'd planned. Daria returned to the conference room where Emma had fallen asleep in Jake's arms and Jake's head lay on top of Emma's. He'd fallen asleep, too. An empty baby food jar lay on the table with drops of pureed carrots decorating it. Emma's lips still had proof of orange leftovers. They had emptied the diaper bag onto the floor, and a wet diaper hung halfway out of the trash can. She suspected he'd tossed it.

She couldn't help but smile. There was enough proof tossed around the room that he had tried to take care of Emma and evidently succeeded.

Daria tapped lightly on Jake's shoulder. His eyes popped open, and he looked up at her. There for a moment, she wanted to lean down and kiss him. She stepped back.

"It's time for us to go to the safe house. McDaniel has a car warming in the back." She smiled at him. "From the looks of this room, you two had a good time. I'll gather everything and help you get her coat on."

"Did you find out anything? What did they say?" Jake sat up.

"We don't have names, but besides the accusations against bank management being involved, there's someone out there still calling the shots."

Jake shuffled Emma in his arms while Daria gently slid the sleeping baby's arms through her coat. He handed her to Daria while he put his coat on. His insides churned. He hadn't been in town long enough to make enemies and yet here he was, still feeling like he was in the war zone.

"Are you ready?" Daria asked. "The safe house is waiting."

"Why not just go back to the hotel? If they're still coming after us, let's face them head-on." Jake exited the building into the cold and slid into the back. He buckled Emma into her car seat and covered her with her blanket. She still gripped the little giraffe.

He hopped out and got in the front with Daria. His fingers were already half-frozen from the short time he'd been exposed to the elements. He rubbed his hands together in front of the air vent, blowing hot air.

"I shouldn't have to answer that question, Jake. You're smart enough to figure it out. Besides, I've been assigned to protect you and Emma, so I must keep my guard up." Daria drove slowly out of the parking lot. "Of course, I've already been keeping a watch on our surroundings since the moment I saw you in the parking lot holding a gun. We've encountered a lot of near-death experiences. I take my job seriously."

"And I listen to my instincts." Jake sat back. "I've already told you I have special training."

"Let's not revisit that conversation." Daria glanced at him. "We've both had training. Now we utilize that knowledge to stay out of the killer's crosshairs. Agreed?"

Jake understood her position, but he sure wanted to leave Emma with Daria while he did his own scouting. She'd made it clear she was the authority. He must abide by the rules, well, unless he saw fit to make some adjustments.

"Agreed." Staying out of sight of the enemy was his goal. Keeping Emma and Daria safe was his priority. He kind of enjoyed having Daria around, even if she was a little bossy. "Why don't we drop Emma off at my parents' house, where she'll be safe?" He tapped the door's armrest with his fingers.

"And put them in danger, too? If only we could place Emma in safe hands, but right now, your hands are the safest. Whoever is watching us may know every move we make. If we leave Emma somewhere, they will think we've left vital information in the same place. We can't risk it."

Jake stared at the car in the distance in front of them. Daria was right. He'd only put others in danger. He tightened his fists and loosened them. The minute Daria had explained the shooters had given up information, he'd sensed the whole takedown was too easy.

"Yeah, bad idea. But you'd think since police have the flash drives, they'd retreat and run." Jake glanced back at Emma. Sound asleep. He stared out of the rear window. "I see your friends are escorting us to our destination. Isn't that a telltale sign to anyone watching that something's going on with three cars caravanning down the street?"

"They are a suitable distance away and the vehicles are different models. It's not like we're chained together. If they were closer, I'd have to agree." Daria turned into a dark driveway, drove around to the back of the house hidden by the forest and stopped.

From the looks of the place, there was no electricity, no streetlight and it was hidden by the trees. How were they supposed to stay warm in a place like this, especially if they were stuck here for a while.

"I know you think that's logical, and this is a small town, but I don't see it in the same way." He turned and faced the front. "Look, one car stops half a block from the house, we turn in and disappear in the forest, while the other car turns in behind us. Tell me that doesn't draw attention."

"Are you insinuating we don't know what we're doing?" Daria's voice rose an octave.

He threw up his hands. "I'm not challenging the police department's procedures. It just seems odd to me. If I were watching for a target overseas, I'd become suspicious if three unknown vehicles approached at the same time." He dropped his hands. "I'm just saying."

Daria rubbed her forehead. "This is what we've always done, and everything turned out fine."

"Okay. I surrender." Jake unbuckled his seat belt. Maybe he was too exhausted to think clearly. Wouldn't be the first time, but he'd never admit it. "What are we waiting for?"

"McDaniel is checking the house out to make sure it's all clear."

Jake would argue the point again. Things didn't feel right, but who was he to push his way of thinking on Daria? Shouldn't the house have been cleared before they got there?

"For your information, there are two officers already inside the house. Smothers and Evans. Cramer will drive away as soon as he gets the all clear from McDaniel."

She appeared confident in their system, so he let it go. Daria's phone lit up with a text.

"It's clear. Let's go." She stepped out of the car. "I'll get the diaper bag. You get Emma."

Jake moved as stealthily as possible and prayed Emma wouldn't cry. Daria met him at the front of the car. They made their way in the dark to the back door. An officer he hadn't met held the door open for them. They entered and stopped in a dark room while the officer closed the back door and locked it behind them, then another officer opened the mudroom door.

Light flooded the place and warmth hit him in the face. "Impressive."

"Jake," Daria said. "This is Officer Smothers and Officer Evans. They will stand watch tonight."

Jake shook their hands, then evaluated the interior of the house. Blackout curtains everywhere. From the outside, it looked like an abandoned house. Who knew it would be cozy and welcoming?

A gas fireplace warmed the living room. Carpet covered the floor, he assumed to keep down the sound of movement inside the house. Oddly, the dragonfly decor wasn't what he'd expected. In the mountains, people normally decorated with deer or bear themes and built log furniture. Not so in here. He liked it.

Daria stood with her hands at her waist. "Do you approve, Mr. Skeptic?"

"Okay, I deserve that." He patted Emma's back. "Where should I lay her down?"

"In here." Daria turned and walked into a small bedroom. "You can put her in here in this porta crib. We'll be able to hear her if she wakes up."

Jake leaned over, placed her on top of a fuzzy, soft yellow blanket and eased her coat off. She rolled over, still asleep. A night-light cast star shadows on the ceiling. *Nice.*

They returned to the living room, and he sat on the sofa in front of the fireplace. For the first time in two days, he relaxed. Daria picked up a tote bag and disappeared into another room. He'd given her a hard time, but she stood her ground and didn't get angry. She'd shown no signs of an anger problem. Raised her voice a time or two, but that's not full-fledged anger. He looked around for the officers. Where'd they go?

Daria entered the room again, only this time wearing a navy police sweatshirt with the side tucked above her weapon, blue jeans, and her feet decked with warm-looking boots. She had let her hair down, and it danced on her shoulders every time she turned her head. Jake caught himself staring.

"What are you looking at?" Daria paused with her eyebrows lifted.

"My best friend from middle school." Jake smiled. "She looks nice."

Daria snickered. "Thanks, but you should meet *my* friend from middle school. He is easy on the eyes." She walked past him to the open kitchen and pulled out two disposable coffee cups. "Can I interest you in a fresh cup?"

"Sure, but I didn't see you bring a bag inside. Did you have clothes already here?"

"No. We keep a change of clothes handy for situations such as this. Evans brought my bag in when he arrived."

"Good thinking." Jake eased from his seat and joined her in the kitchen. He had an urge to wrap his arms around her but backed off. She must have sensed something because she had a questioning look on her face. He reached for the empty cup about the time she dropped a coffee pod into the coffee maker. Their hands touched. Their eyes met.

Jake set his cup down. "Excuse me. I'm getting in the way." He pointed to the small kitchen table. Why was he suddenly nervous? "I... I'll just sit over here and wait."

"It only takes a minute. These instant coffee makers are the greatest thing since microwaves." Her voice sounded a little shaken.

Awkward. We'd been the best of friends. Why am I so uncomfortable?

Best change the subject. "Where are your friends? I haven't seen them."

"Evans is keeping an eye out from the back entrance where it's dark. Smothers will roam from room to room to monitor the windows and listen for unusual noises." She placed two cups of hot coffee on the table and sat down.

Jake took a quick sip from his cup. "What's the plan?" He tapped the table with his finger and tried to focus on the situation at hand and not on his beautiful, brown-eyed bodyguard or partner or whatever she was. He must reel in his admiration of her. She was a smart lady. She'd figure it out if she hadn't already.

She held her coffee with both hands and placed her elbows on the table. "As long as we have an uneventful night, I'm working on a safe and more comfortable place for you and Emma to stay until this case is resolved and your house is repaired."

"And where might that be?" Jake studied her. Where would be safer than the safe house? "This place is nice enough."

"I know. We've worked hard to keep it a secret, but one never knows—"

A loud noise sounded at the back door.

Jake darted out of the chair and faced the door. Daria jumped to her feet with her weapon drawn, and Smothers stood in the middle of the room in a ready stance with his weapon in hand.

EIGHT

Daria edged to the mudroom door. Her hand slowly turned the knob to the small entrance door where Evans held up. The uncertain sound of scuffling had her ready for the intruder. Smothers moved closer and tried to get Jake to back off. Jake backed to the opposite side from her, took her hand from the doorknob and motioned he would open the door on the count of three. She and Smothers could surprise whoever had overtaken the officer. Her rapid pulse sent adrenaline racing through her body.

She exchanged glances with her coworker and nodded her head in agreement. Jake held up three fingers, then counted down. Three, two, one. He jerked the door open. Daria aimed her weapon, lowered it and burst out laughing. Smothers relaxed his stance and laughed. Daria turned her focus on Jake, laughing. His laughter hadn't changed. She liked the sound of it.

Evans, who was supposed to watch the rear entrance, had knocked over a box of cleaning supplies and a mixture of cleaning liquids had spilled on the floor, making the floor slippery. His foot slipped every time he moved, and it sounded like a fight going on.

"Now that I've entertained everyone, somebody help me up," Evans said. "I don't think anyone will come through here tonight."

Jake reached his muscular arm out and, with one quick tug, Evans almost flew through the kitchen. He kicked off his shoes and turned to Jake.

"Remind me not to make you angry." Evans brushed at his soaked pants. "At least it smells good."

Daria sat back down in her chair, still chuckling, and picked up her coffee. "I've got to hand it to you, Evans. You sure know how to entertain."

"I'd say he successfully tested our reflexes." Jake scooted his chair back in place and slurped his coffee.

"Good thing he'd brought a change of clothes." Daria shook her head and held back more laughter. Of all the unexpected occurrences during a serious situation, this one ranked at the top. Evans picked up a small bag from the corner of the room and disappeared into the bathroom.

Smothers grabbed himself a cup of coffee and returned to his post roaming the house, keeping watch. Evans emerged from the bathroom in a slightly wrinkled uniform. He tossed a few towels on the mudroom floor from the entrance to the kitchen doorway. He picked up the strewn bottles and glass cleaners, then threw another towel down and closed the door.

"That was one of the funniest bloopers I've ever seen a police officer do." Jake's smile covered his face. A real smile, like old times.

"I'm sure he's embarrassed. He's not one who goofs around." Daria yawned. "Want to move to the living room and enjoy the fireplace?"

"Thought you'd never ask." Jake took his coffee with him. "I've been eyeing the recliner since we walked in the door."

Daria curled her legs up under her on the sofa. Its softness consoled her weary body. "So, why didn't you write me or call after your family moved away?"

Jake's jaw dropped. "Did you seriously expect a middle schooler to communicate? I never liked reading until I was in high school, and my writing wasn't legible. Still isn't."

"I guess not." She pulled the gray blanket off the back of the sofa and covered her legs. "I thought about you a lot after you left. I wrote to you, but I'm not sure I had the correct address. Do you plan to stay in Kimbleton, or will you sell your sister's house and move away?"

Jake pulled the footrest up on the recliner and leaned back almost flat. "Kimbleton is home to Emma and me. Besides, my parents are here. I want to be close to my family."

"Good. I'm glad you're back." She turned sideways on the sofa, still sitting up, and rested her head on the soft fabric. "Maybe we can walk the mountain trails together once this case is closed."

A snore met her ears. He hadn't heard her. Just as well. She tossed the blanket off and went to check on Emma. Amazingly, she'd slept through all the commotion. She'd rolled over onto her tummy and pulled her arms and legs up under her. Poor baby. She needed a good night's sleep. Daria readjusted her blanket and tucked it snug around her little body. She'd always loved children, but Emma held a special place in her heart.

Daria tiptoed around the house to check in with

Smothers and Evans before she returned to the sofa. She spotted Evans on his phone.

"Love you, too." Evans slid his cell into his pocket. "Had to check on Karla, you know, my wife. She hasn't been feeling well. A bug, I guess."

"I hope she gets to feeling better. Is everything okay back here?"

"Quiet for now." Evans turned back and checked the window.

Daria returned to the living room where light snores continued at a steady pace from her tough marine. Her marine? She liked the sound of calling him hers.

"You need to quit roaming and get some rest while you can. That shoulder of yours needs a break." Jake's unexpected comment caused her to jump.

"I thought you were asleep. You were snoring." She settled back into her relaxed position.

"It's a gift, I guess, after being on active duty." Jake never opened his eyes. "I sleep, but I'm aware of what's going on around me. Thanks for checking in on Emma."

Daria stared at Jake lying there relaxed and half asleep. It was a blessing that he knew her whereabouts, but a little strange. She yawned and laid her head back.

"You're welcome." Her words slid out in a whisper. She closed her eyes, allowing herself to sink into the soft cushion and sleep.

A shot fired. Jake and Daria jumped to their feet. Smothers ran into the living room from one direction with his weapon still holstered and Evans ran in from the back with his weapon drawn.

"It's okay. Some guy just shot a deer. I saw him in his orange vest and rifle in the distance." Smothers backed away. "Get some more rest if you can. The sun is just on the horizon."

Emma whined.

"She's probably wet and hungry." Daria pulled out a diaper from Emma's bag. "We're going to have to get more diapers soon. There are only two more. She needs milk, too, not just juice." Daria held the fresh diaper in the air. "Do you want to do the honors, or do you want me to?"

Jake's grin said it all. "I'll let you do it. I know you like babies." He sat back down in the recliner.

"I figured you'd say that." She grabbed Emma a change of clothes, too.

Emma sat up in the porta crib, rubbing her eyes. She stretched her arms out to Daria. *Precious.* Most babies just waking up are ready to be cuddled. She'd soaked through her clothes. Daria placed her on the nearby bed and handed her the nearly empty sippy cup until she could get her changed.

She pooched her lips out and shook her empty cup. Full-blown cries filled the house. Jake appeared at the bedroom door in a flash. Daria picked her up and handed her to Jake.

"What's wrong with her?" Jake's wide eyes and confused look tickled her as he followed her through the house. "What do I do? I haven't heard her cry like this before."

"And it won't be the last time." Daria went into the kitchen in search of some milk. "She's hungry and her cup is empty."

"Oh, is that all?" He sat at the table, holding Emma.

She screamed louder and stiffened. "Are you sure she's not hurting?"

Daria searched for milk but couldn't find anything except for the coffee creamer. "Looks like she'll have to have this coffee creamer. We don't have milk. Good thing you like your coffee black."

She poured the creamer into the sippy cup, all the while Emma fought with Jake, reaching her hands out for her cup. Daria tightened the lid and handed the cup to her. She leaned back on Jake's chest, satisfied.

Jake's eyebrows lifted. "I don't act like that when I'm hungry."

"I sure hope not." Daria grinned and shook her head. Jake had a lot to learn about taking care of a baby. However, she admired how gentle this tough marine was with Emma. It only showed he had a soft side to his rough exterior.

Evans and Smothers entered the kitchen.

"Looks like a hunters club has arrived. They've gathered in the woods behind the house," Evans said. "At least, I hope that's where they're from. But I don't like it. There's too many to monitor."

Smothers spoke up. "Same here. I saw them walking around to the back of the house. Could be harmless, but I'd suggest we pack up and leave for safety's sake."

"I don't have anything to pack up except for a diaper bag." Jake held Emma close. "Well, maybe putting on her coat and wrapping her in the blanket."

"You take care of her." Daria went toward the bedroom. "I'll get her things and grab my bag."

An unsettled feeling knotted in Daria's stomach. Were they hunters or did they have a part in the illegal activity in town? Would they surround the house? Surely, they wouldn't harm Emma.

She stuffed everything in the diaper bag, including the little giraffe. Daria paused in the living room and put on her coat before helping Jake put Emma's coat on her. Emma wouldn't let go of her cup. Jake pulled it from her hand, and she let out a squeal. He handed it back after getting her coat on. He handed her off to Daria and put his coat on, then took her back into his arms.

"Is it always like this when she's hungry?" Jake wrapped the blanket around her.

"Not always. But you must realize, she's only had one decent meal. Didn't you put a small box of dry cereal in that zipped side pocket yesterday? Give that to her. Maybe it will suffice for a bit. She was definitely hungry. Enough so that she didn't balk over coffee creamer."

Smothers paused at the mudroom door. "Are you ready? Let's make this quick. Evans will go out before you. Cramer and McDaniel are at the edge of the woods to help cover you in case something goes wrong."

The old racing pulse hit Daria instantly. Why were these hunters right here, right now?

Jake and Daria didn't waste any time getting into their car. Daria started the car and backed out as fast as she could, planning on a fast getaway. Four hunters aimed their rifles toward her vehicle.

Smothers, Cramer and McDaniel engaged in gunfire, turning the men's attention to them so Daria could get away. A bullet pinged her door before she could drive off.

Her car slid on the ice.

* * *

"Go, go…" Jake sat sideways with one hand on the dash and one hand on the back of the seat. Emma wasn't bothered by the shots. Her cereal and sippy cup had her occupied.

"I've got it." Daria straightened and maintained control of the vehicle.

An unmarked car pulled beside them, blocking them from the shooters. Evans threw up his hand and pointed forward. Wherever he'd parked, he'd shielded them in record time. Jake decided Evans had redeemed himself from his slippery fall in the entryway.

Daria slowed when she reached the main part of town. She merged into the morning tourist traffic. Lines of cars overflowed into the street as people waited their turn in the diner's drive-through.

Jake took in a deep sniff. "Mmm, gotta love the smell of bacon."

"It's coming from the mom-and-pop place on the left." She pulled into the other lane and passed a slow driver. "We can't risk it."

"Don't tell me," Jake said. "Are we going back to the station where it's *safe*?" He made quotation marks with his fingers. "We could go back to my house. I know how to barricade us in and watch for the enemy."

Daria huffed. "Jake…"

"I know, I know. I'm not in Afghanistan anymore. But it would work. Prepare and draw them in." He found himself amused at harassing her with his antics about the war. He liked the way her nose curled up at his humorous thoughts.

"I'm meeting with Jeffers to discuss an alternative

plan. Julia, our administrative assistant, has already called for a full breakfast delivery to the station." Daria stopped at a red light.

"Now, that's what I'm talking about. Prompt service." Jake tapped the armrest with his fingers. He tensed, sitting in the heavy traffic with unknowns all around them.

He zeroed in on different cars and studied their behavior. Emma sat glassy-eyed with her head leaned against the headrest of her car seat, her hand still looped around the handle of her sippy cup, remnants of cereal sprinkled on her coat and a streak of escaped coffee creamer at the side of her mouth. If only Amanda could see her now. If only he could see his sister right now.

Daria turned on a side road and then into the back parking lot of the department. She glanced over and smiled at him.

"In case you haven't figured it out, we will change vehicles again when we leave." She stopped at the back entrance. "Let's go inside. One of the guys will change out the cars and install her car seat."

Jake stepped out and made sure his feet wouldn't slip on the frozen pavement before he unbuckled Emma. She came to life and started kicking, reaching her arms out to him. Amazing the rush of warmth that overtook him, knowing Emma wanted him. He pulled her out and held her close. Her arms wrapped around his neck with her sippy cup dangling by two fingers.

"Bite," she said.

"In a minute. Food is waiting for us." Jake spoke into her ear. Her little curls tickled his nose. "You just had cereal. Are you still hungry?"

Once again, the well-heated station was a pleasant relief from the freezing temperatures outside. Since he'd been there several times, he knew the way to the conference room, so he didn't wait for Daria to give him instructions.

"Where are you going?" Daria shut the door and made sure the automatic lock clicked closed.

"To the conference room. Where else?"

She pointed to a different hallway. "We're going this way where there are no windows."

"Because?"

"To cut down on visibility and glass."

"And random shootings. Got it." Jake lifted his eyebrows and stepped into a smaller room with a table and four chairs. Nothing like the well-decorated conference room. The aroma of bacon hit his nostrils. He smiled and winked at Daria. "Somebody knows how to order a breakfast." A small coffee maker with different flavors of coffee pods sat on a built-in shelf.

Emma's plate was obvious by its flower shape and divided compartments. It looked rather festive with all the food placed in sections. It contained a cup of strawberries, small pieces of toast, pieces of cheese and more dry cereal. He spotted two half-pints of milk nearby.

The three of them enjoyed their bountiful breakfast and had a moment to relax after their harrowing morning. Jake sighed. Everyone was alive and well, and that's what counted.

"I'll be back in a few minutes." Daria opened the door and paused. "I've got to meet with Jeffers." She spun and closed the door behind her.

Jake picked at the remains of breakfast. He could've

devoured a whole pound of crispy bacon, but the four pieces he'd had served their purpose and were delicious. Emma took bites of her strawberries. She played with some and smeared them on the table like painting a picture.

He recounted all the near-death misses he'd encountered since arriving in town. None of his marine buddies would believe he was battling an enemy in the US. He couldn't believe it himself. All he wanted was a quiet life with his little niece and maybe Daria if she'd have him.

Emma pointed to a group picture of police officers on the wall. "Da-da."

"I don't think that's your daddy." He studied the picture and noted Daria standing in the middle. She'd made a name for herself, and he was certain this case would earn her the respect she was due.

Daria stepped back into the room. She popped another pod into the coffee maker. "I met with Jeffers. He said officers caught Gregory Hall trying to leave town." Her coffee finished, she pulled out the chair and sat down. "First, Gregory said he was going on a trip for the holidays. Then, he changed his story and said his life was in danger."

Jake joined her with a fresh cup of the hot brew. "Sounds like he's hiding something. Why would anyone want him dead if he's calling the shots? All the coded records were on his computer."

"That's just it. He insisted we don't know who we're dealing with." She took a drink. "Honestly, that's the truth. We *don't* know who we're dealing with. If it's not bank staff, what are we missing?"

His gut churned. Who was playing games with them?

Taunting them everywhere they went. Could it be an inside job? He'd only just arrived in town a couple of days ago.

Daria reached over and lightly squeezed Jake's arm. "I've lined up a place for you and Emma to stay. It's the safest place I know outside of the police station."

Jake lifted his eyes to her. "And where might that be since nowhere else seems to fit the bill?"

She smiled that familiar caring smile. "My brother's house. Robert is an investigator with the department now. I'm sure you remember him. He has a garage apartment that he rents out to vacationers, and right now there's no one staying there. You and Emma are welcome to stay as long as you like. He's looking forward to catching up on old times."

"What if trouble finds us? Won't we be putting him in danger?" Jake hesitated. He didn't want to involve anyone else and risk someone dying in his place.

"No. Trust me. He's already making plans for your arrival."

"Who am I to argue? Emma and I will do as you say." *As long as I agree.* Jake pushed to his feet. "Let's go. I'm ready to see another one of my old friends."

"Okay, give me a minute. I've got to make sure the car is ready and we're clear to leave." Daria took the last drink of her coffee and dropped the disposable cup in the trash. She left the room again.

Jake gathered the trash from their breakfast delivery and tossed most of it in the small trash can. He found a napkin and wiped Emma's hands and mouth. "A wet rag would be better, but this will have to do."

He set her on the floor and watched her toddle around

the room. She slapped the chair's cushion and jabbered indecipherable words. So strange for him to tower over this little human and for her to walk with such short legs. Jake admired her cuteness. She made her way around the table and back to him. Her arms draped around his leg. He reached down, picked her up and kissed her rosy cheeks, then ruffled her hair.

"You are too cute for your own good. But you probably know that. My guess is your mama told you multiple times a day." He glanced at the clock, then back at Emma. "If Daria doesn't return soon, it will be time to eat again."

The door flew open. "Okay, we're all set." She put her coat on.

Jake did the same and bundled Emma up. "Hold on." He filled both of her sippy cups with the half-pints of milk. "Should've done that before now, but she had her juice." He smiled at Daria and walked out with Emma in his arms.

It hadn't warmed up much during their breakfast, but with the bright sun beaming down, Jake knew some of the ice would melt on the roads, especially with the added tourist traffic. The drive to her brother's house wouldn't be so treacherous. They got into the car and drove away.

"Is your brother married?" Jake enjoyed the drive through his old mountain home place. People were out hanging tinsel and Christmas decor along the main part of town.

"Yes. He married Gina, but you may not know her. She moved into town the same summer you moved away. They have two children. A boy, Isaac, eight years old, and a girl, Alexa, six."

Her cheerful tone had him almost forgetting they were still on the hit list from an unknown enemy. His nerves were a bit on edge. He must keep his eyes open, his marine intelligence intact and be ready for anything.

NINE

Daria relaxed the moment she pulled into Robert and Gina's driveway. Home away from home and filled with love. The moment they stepped out of the car, Alexa and Isaac met them. They'd been sliding in the snow and had already heard a baby was moving into the garage apartment. They were excited to see her, especially Alexa. She jumped up and down and clapped her gloved hands.

Robert opened the front door and greeted Jake with a handshake. "Hey, man, it's great to see you after all these years. Come on in. Gina has lunch ready. She even had me get the high chair out of the attic for Emma."

Daria made her way into the kitchen where Gina was pouring fresh glasses of iced tea. "We're here. I have someone I want you to meet. Well, two someones." She laughed. "This is the Jake Fisher you've already heard about. And this little doll is Emma."

Gina held her hands out to Emma. She willingly fell into Gina's arms, who turned and put her in the high chair with all kinds of snacks on the tray. Emma squealed and picked at her food.

Everyone sat at the table and talked about old times

over a delicious pot roast lunch with all the fixings. Despite all the noise and conversation going on between Jake and Robert, Emma fell asleep. Daria's eyes rolled as weariness caught up with her.

Gina placed her hand on Daria's arm. "These guys can talk for hours. You look exhausted. Why don't you go catch a nap on the couch? I'll take care of Emma."

Daria excused herself and moved to the living room. Her body seemed to understand it was going to rest in a safe place. The minute her head touched the cushion, everything went silent.

Laughter from the distance bolted her to her feet. She'd slept too long. The setting sun made the twinkling lights on Robert's Christmas tree dance brighter, and the fragrance of his fresh tree reminded her it was the season she loved so much.

Daria followed the voices to the dim sunroom. Emma sat content in Jake's lap. Robert and Gina sat on the sofa facing a foot of freshly fallen snow. The entire scene was a peaceful, heartwarming sight.

"I didn't mean to sleep this late. My apologies." Daria entered the room. "Have you shown Jake the garage apartment?"

"No. Thought we'd let you do the honors," Robert said. "By the way, Jake, I figured you'd be about my size, so I set out some clean clothes for you. Hope they fit."

Jake stood, holding Emma. "I've enjoyed catching up, and I appreciate having a place to stay." He faced Daria. "Okay, show me my quarters." He placed his hand on her back.

She drew in a breath at his touch. "Sure, but everyone still needs to put on their coats."

In a matter of minutes, Daria unlocked the garage apartment. He roamed around, checking things out. Daria went into the spare room and turned down the cover on the toddler bed. She took drowsy Emma from Jake, changed her clothes and laid her in bed with a soft stuffed teddy bear and her sippy cup, then covered her up.

Emma shuffled her legs but didn't offer to get up. Daria turned to leave the room. Jake stood in the doorway, watching her. He walked over and kissed Emma's head. Little hands lifted and touched his cheeks, and she lifted her head and kissed him on the nose.

Daria's heart melted at the precious moment she'd just witnessed. She backed away and waited for Jake in the living room. He stepped out and pulled Emma's door almost closed.

"She kissed me. Can you believe it?" Jake's eyes widened. "I hope to make my sister proud."

"You are already. Now you need to get some rest. I'll see you in the morning." She zipped her coat. "Jeffers told me to take a few days off to let my shoulder heal. Maybe we can all get some much-needed rest."

She walked to the front door and reached for the doorknob, then turned back. "Good night, Jake." His eyes captured hers. Was she reading his expression correctly?

He stepped closer. "Do you think we can renew our friendship?"

"I think after the past couple of days, we already have." Was he thinking what she was thinking? She needed to hear him say it.

"What I mean is, can we renew our friendship and see where it leads?" He shuffled his stance. "I realize we've only just reconnected, but it seems like yesterday we were racing across the playground toward the swings."

Robert stepped out on the side porch. The door slammed behind him and the noise disturbed their conversation. Robert walked over to his truck.

Daria looked back at Jake. "Get some rest, Jake. Robert will stand guard tonight. We'll talk tomorrow." She walked away before she made a hasty decision. He needed to sleep on it and see if he still felt the same in the morning. She didn't want the turbulence of their day and the emotions involved to sway his thinking or hers. But they were both protectors and made a great team in her eyes.

She got in her car and waved as she drove away. Home was calling her name. Robert and Gina wanted her to stay the night, but she longed for the comforts of home. Her whole routine had turned into a nightmare. The sun had set and the evening hours dropped the temperature below freezing. The slick roads made travel treacherous, but she made it home.

In a matter of minutes, she'd prepared for bed, then crawled in and pulled the covers to her chin. Thoughts of the past two days rolled through her head. Relieved Jake and Emma were safe at her brother's, she could get some undisturbed rest and continue her investigation tomorrow. If only her mind would shut down.

Had the threatening text she'd received come from the unknown ringleader? The bank president seemed to fit the position, but evidently there was someone higher pulling the strings.

Every time she closed her eyes, Jake's dark brown

eyes stared back at her. The seriousness of his gaze mesmerized her. Made her feel like a kid again. Concern about the case had her stumped.

A creak in her kitchen popped her eyes wide open. She slid out of bed, paused and listened. Someone was in her house. She secured her weapon and eased out of her bedroom and into the hallway. The intruder's steps drew closer while the lights of her Christmas tree in the living room formed a silhouette on the wall of a person inching her way. She readied her stance with weapon in hand and flipped the light switch on. Nothing happened.

God, help me.

The figure moved closer. She sensed him close but couldn't see in the darkness. A hard object hit her head. She dropped to the floor, lying partly on her weapon. Her ears rang relentlessly. Pain shot through her sore shoulder and head. Footsteps, two sets, scrambled around her. One of the intruders flipped her over on top of her weapon. They must not have seen it. Would they finish her? She barely opened her eyes and struggled not to grimace as the ache in her shoulder intensified. From what she could tell in the dark, they both wore ski masks.

"We proved our point," a deep voice said. "Should we take her out?"

"No. We were instructed to scare her. Probably knocked her out. Next time she dies," the other man said. The smooth tone in his voice sounded familiar.

They rushed away. The front door slammed shut.

Were they gone or were they coming back? *Who were they?*

She fumbled under her hip for her pistol, then pushed

to her feet, falling against the wall. Her staggering feet made it difficult to move fast. She made it back to her bedroom, grabbed her cell and fell across her bed as she punched in 911. All went silent.

The distant sound of voices invaded the ringing in her ears and caused her to stir. Someone called her name. Help had arrived.

"Daria, where are you?" Footsteps rushed through her house and into her bedroom, with flashlights searching the room. "Here she is."

Her head throbbed. The police had arrived, and she was safe. Tears escaped.

McDaniel leaned over her. "Are you okay? Who did this?" He turned away. "Get the paramedic in here, stat."

She moaned, then pushed slowly to a sitting position and thought her head would explode. Two paramedics came in with their equipment and a gurney. They had her lie back. She swayed. Strong hands helped her lie down.

"Evans, call her brother, Robert. You've got his number, don't you?" McDaniel said.

"Got it." Evans's voice faded as he left the room.

Daria squinted at everyone surrounding her, holding flashlights. Were there really that many people in front of her, or was she seeing double? She was coherent, but everyone seemed far away. "I… I'm gonna be sick." The room spun.

"Here, take this." A paramedic handed her a bag, just in case.

More strong arms picked her up and placed her on the gurney, covering her with a blanket. Cold air hit her face, increasing the strength of the headache. They loaded her into the ambulance. Once at the hospital, another familiar face looked down at her. The same doctor she'd seen earlier. He checked her eyes and felt around on her head, then ordered a CT scan.

"Can you tell me what happened?" the doctor asked.

McDaniel stood at the corner of the room with his lips drawn tight.

She explained the shadow she'd seen before the lights went out. She'd only seen one shadow but heard two sets of feet shuffle around her. They wore ski masks. There was no way to make a positive ID.

The technician came in and wheeled her to radiology, then returned her to her room in the emergency department. It didn't surprise Daria when he told her she had a concussion and needed to rest for a few days, and she still needed to take it easy on that shoulder. She'd already planned on resting, but not under doctor's orders after being assaulted in her own home.

The door to her ER room opened and Robert ran in, glanced at her and turned to McDaniel. "What happened? I got here as soon as I could."

Jake stepped past Robert. She reached her hand out to him. He rushed to her side and took her hand, then put his other hand tenderly against her cheek. "I'm so glad you're okay. We'll find out who did this."

It was all Jake could do to maintain control of his anger. If anyone had an anger problem, it was him. And if he could get his hands on whoever attacked her, well, it wouldn't be nice. Standing there looking at her, he realized his feelings were more than friendship. If anything had happened to her, it would have devastated him.

After the doctor discharged her from the hospital, Robert and Jake helped her into Robert's truck. Jake put his arm around her so she could lean on him. Why was someone after her? Was it to keep her from protecting him and Emma? The flash drives were in police hands, as were the two shooters. Whoever broke into her home must know that by now. So, was there something else these intruders were looking for?

They pulled into Robert's driveway. Gina flipped the front porch light on and opened the door.

"Is she okay? I've got the guest room ready for her." Gina stepped out into the cold and held the door open for them.

Jake picked Daria up. She wrapped her arms around his neck and leaned her head against his chest. His emotions soared. He placed her on the bed in the guest room. Gina stepped beside him, as did Robert.

Daria blinked and looked up at them. "Hey, I'm okay. Just have a monster headache. Thank you for everything."

"The doctor said you need to rest and limit activities for a few days." Jake searched her face. She'd been through a traumatic ordeal.

"I'll be okay. You guys don't need to look so worried." She placed her hand over her eyes. "Could you turn the light off? It hurts my eyes."

"Okay." Jake kissed her hand. "If you need anything, just say so." He stepped back while Gina covered her up.

Everyone left the room. Jake paused in the doorway. Should he sit in the corner chair in case she needed something during the night? Was it safe to leave her there alone?

"Jake," Robert called out to him. "Come on, man. She'll be okay and she's safe here, as are you and Emma."

Jake closed her door and had to pull himself away. Out of all the situations he'd been through overseas and in the US, he felt the tug, like a magnet, to protect her. He went into the kitchen, where it seemed everyone always gathered. Robert sat at the table with a glass of water.

"It's after 1:00 a.m. We all need to go to bed and get some rest." Robert took a gulp of his drink. "I want to talk to Daria and see what she remembers, but I'll wait until morning." He downed the rest of his water and stood. "I'm calling it a night. We will find who did this."

"Good night." Jake pondered his next move. Should he go to his garage apartment or sit in the hall at Daria's door? Emma slept soundly in Robert and Gina's master bedroom, so he didn't have to worry about her.

The house fell quiet while Jake struggled with leaving the house. He went into the living room and sat on the sofa. Sleep evaded him. His brain wouldn't shut down after almost losing Daria. He sat there for what seemed like hours before easing down the hallway and sitting on the floor by her door. He laid his head back against the wall and relaxed. That was it. He needed to be closer to her.

He'd only just closed his eyes when a nudge from a boot moved his leg. Jake jumped to his feet. "What's wrong?" He blinked to clear his vision after being in a deep sleep.

"Nothing's wrong," Robert said. "Half the morning's gone. Thought you might want some coffee to get you going."

Jake looked back at Daria's door, then joined Robert in the kitchen where Emma sat in the high chair with milk around her mouth and her hands in oatmeal. Gina stood over the stove frying bacon. It smelled wonderful. He spotted their two children out in the backyard building a snowman.

"Why didn't you wake me sooner?" Jake rubbed his eyes.

"You were out of it, and you needed the rest or whatever rest you get by sitting on the floor," Robert chuckled. "We understood, though. It's no secret how you feel about her. We've noticed the way you two look at each other."

A noise down the hall caught Jake's attention. He almost knocked the chair over, jumping up to check on Daria. She'd emerged from her room. He eased up, kissed her on the forehead and wrapped his arms around her. He could hold her forever.

She reciprocated his hug, then pushed away. "Where is everyone?" Her soft tone alerted him that her head still hurt.

"In the kitchen. I don't have to tell you Gina's cooking bacon. You can smell it all over the house." He took her hand and walked with her down the hall. "How are you this morning?"

"My head still hurts, but I'm okay. The ache in my shoulder has subsided." Her slow movement showed differently. She dropped his hand as they joined her family at the table.

Gina rushed to her side and hugged her. "Good morning. I fixed your coffee. I'm so sorry about last night. So horrifying."

Robert sat back in his chair, eyeing her. Jake could tell the wheels were turning in Robert's mind and he was giving Daria time to wake up. Gina set some biscuits on the table.

"Eat up, everyone. I've already fed the kids and sent them out to play to keep the noise down for Daria." Gina joined them at the table. She bowed her head. "Dear God, thank You for this food we are about to receive. Continue to heal Daria and keep everyone safe. Amen."

Robert cleared his throat. Jake wondered when he'd chime in and start questioning Daria. "Sis, do you remember any other details about last night's intruders?"

"There were no real details." Daria straightened her shoulders. "There was a noise in the kitchen, the Christmas lights were on, a single silhouette cast on the wall, but for only a second before the house went dark. I eased down my hall and someone knocked me over the head. I wasn't unconscious, but they thought I was. He rolled me over, and suddenly I was aware of two people stomping through my house, then out the front door. That's it."

"Have you had any encounters with anyone lately that would cause them to come after you?" Robert took a quick slurp of his coffee and set the cup down.

Jake spoke up. "Since I arrived in town, there's been nothing but attacks on Emma, Daria and me. Mainly me. I suppose they are after Daria now, since she's been assigned protective duty over us."

"None that I'm aware of, Robert." Daria bit off a piece of bacon, irritated with the way Jake answered for her. "Some of the guys at the station have been giving me a hard time over that arrest I did a while back.

They all call me a hothead, but they wouldn't do anything this drastic."

"So there's no one who stands out as particularly suspicious?" Robert continued. "I know your head hurts, but I need you to think."

Jake sat at the edge of his seat over Robert's questioning. If he had something to say, Jake wanted to hear it. "What is it you're getting at, Robert? Spit it out."

Daria placed her fork on the table and turned her eyes on her brother. "What are you trying to tell us?"

Robert leaned back, looked around and drew in a deep breath. His hesitance to speak increased the tension in the room. Jake shifted his eyes from Daria, to Robert, to Gina, and back to Robert.

"I've been an investigator for the department for eight years now, and I've never encountered a situation like we have now. Regarding your case with the embezzlement and the flash drives, I'm highly suspicious we have a leak in the department. Apparently, all these continuous attacks are because of another piece of evidence that came up missing from the bank, specifically Gregory Hall's office." Robert placed his hand on Daria's shoulder. She winced. "You guys need to watch your backs and be cautious."

Daria shrugged her shoulder out from under Robert's hand. She placed her elbows on the table and leaned her head in her hands. "I don't get it. We turned in all the flash drives." She turned her head toward Jake. Her weak eyes stared into his eyes. "What piece of evidence are we missing? Another flash drive? What?"

Jake lifted his hands and shook his head. "I have no clue. I've been gone for years. I don't know what belongs to Tom and Amanda and what doesn't. We can search the house again if you want."

"Yes. We need to do that." Daria scooted from the table.

Gina touched her arm. "Honey, you've been through enough. You need to rest like the doctor ordered."

"Killers don't rest, Gina." Daria stood. "They won't stop until they've completed their job. I'll be fine after I take a couple of those over-the-counter pain relievers."

"First things first. Daria, I know how determined you are. If you insist on pressing forward in your condition, Jake will have to watch after you." Robert tossed his truck keys on the table. "Jake, you can drive my truck and take Daria to the station so she can file her report. Gina said she'd be happy to watch Emma while you're gone."

Jake picked up the keys and stood. "I've learned in the past few days that when she sets her mind on something, there's no changing it."

"You learn fast." Robert slapped Jake on the back.

"I'm going to the apartment to clean up while Daria gets ready. Thank you for a delicious breakfast and for all of your hospitality." He exited the house and went to his temporary quarters.

Had Amanda hidden more evidence? Was it even her at all? Had someone else caught on to what his sister had involved herself in and become greedy, trying to blackmail bank staff? Would he know the item if he saw it?

TEN

Daria made her way to the shower after Gina gave her two pain relievers. She closed her eyes while the hot water beat against her shoulders. A flash of a man's dress shoe near her head popped up so vividly she let out a quick scream. She couldn't tell what color the shoe was, but the shape of it she'd seen before, somewhere.

Her headache calmed down some. She finished her shower and dressed, then went to go talk to Robert. He was her brother, after all, and they worked for the same police department. Gina pointed her toward his home office. Daria knocked as she entered.

"Hey, do you have a minute?" She sat in the chair in front of his desk.

"Sure. What's up?" He leaned back in his leather desk chair and crossed his legs. "Did you remember something?"

"How'd you know?"

"It's not unusual for victims to remember more details after a few hours or even a few days." He smiled at her. "What have you got?"

She explained being in the shower and the flash popping into her head. "I've seen that style of shoe before, but I can't remember who wears them."

"That's good. While you're out today, not following doctor's orders, pay attention to people's shoes. Especially people you know. Maybe something will click."

She stood and walked to his doorway. "I will. See you soon."

"Take care of my truck." Robert's voice echoed down the hall.

Jake met her in the living room, tossing the keys in the air and catching them. He looked handsome in Robert's black jeans and blue pullover sweater.

"I'm ready." She patted her side. Her pistol sat housed in her holster.

Jake walked her to the passenger side of the truck and opened her door. His hand touched the small of her back, steadying her as she stepped in and buckled up.

"Thanks." Daria rubbed her forehead.

God, thank You for sparing my life.

Jake slid into the driver's side and gripped the steering wheel, obviously admiring Robert's truck. "Now, this is what I'm talking about. A real truck."

They backed out of the driveway and eased down the partially thawed road. The sun had melted spots here and there. Jake appeared in deep thought.

"Something on your mind?" She put on sunglasses. The bright sun bouncing off the crystalline snow felt like a spotlight in her eyes, increasing the dull headache.

"When I heard someone assaulted you, my heart stopped. I had to get to you and make sure you were okay. I haven't had the best attitude since we reconnected. It's not you. It's me and it's not a cop-out. I've blamed myself for my comrade's death. I was supposed to throw that grenade. My commanding officer approved the change and allowed my friend to toss it instead. He became a casualty of war while I lived to be here today." Jake turned the corner and pulled down his visor. "After all that's happened, I prayed and surrendered those hurts to God. I finally realized the guilt over his death wasn't mine to carry. My friend volunteered and knew the risks. He was a great guy. He gave his all for our country."

"Jake, I don't know what to say other than I'm sorry you and your buddies had to go through that battle and lose friends in the process. God is faithful to take over and help us find peace." She laid her head back on the headrest. "Since this is confession time, I must admit that I could have handled my actions toward that disorderly vacationer differently. My duty was to protect other tourists from his unacceptable behavior in public. Maybe my arrest was a little hasty, but he had become more disruptive and obnoxious."

She stared out of the passenger side window and sighed. "My goal is to prove myself a good cop in control of her temper, find the ones responsible for killing Amanda and Tom and be the best friend a friend can have." Her eyes shifted to Jake.

She may have been off kilter last night after going to the hospital, but she remembered his gentle embrace. "I'm glad to know you surrendered to God because I rededicated my life to Him last night. He's given me a whole new outlook on life, and I don't have to answer to anyone but Him."

Jake stopped at the red light. His silence told her he

was deep in thought. Maybe all this confession was too much, but since they'd started, she wanted to finish and be clearheaded.

"Another thing." She rubbed her forehead and placed her hand on the seat beside her. Jake's warm hand covered hers and squeezed lightly, then let go.

"What's that?" His compassionate eyes hit her like an arrow of love to the heart. The light changed again, and they continued their journey down the road and through the last leg of the forest toward the station.

"My career is no longer my passion. I'm looking for something more out of life." Her pulse increased as she held her breath for his response.

He slowed with the traffic, stopped at the light and stared straight ahead. Was he going to respond? Had she put him on the spot? She'd wanted to unload everything while she had the chance.

He shifted and faced her. "I meant what I said in the early hours this morning before the assault. As a scrawny kid, years ago I thought you were the best friend ever. It wasn't until seeing you again that I realized my best friend could be my soulmate." He held her hand in both of his.

Tears escaped, her head pounded and her lip quivered. "I prayed before going to bed last night that you meant what you said. As a kid, I understood the feeling of friendship. Maybe that's why I could date no one around town. No one compared to you."

Jake leaned across the seat and kissed her lightly. She returned the kiss but pushed away and sat back.

"When you moved away, my world caved. I thought I'd lost you forever. Maybe God's working His plan for us now, but I don't want to move too fast. A lot of things have happened through the years, and now you have Emma. You might need—"

"Is Emma a problem?" Jake's lips tightened.

"No, that's not what I meant."

Now what have I done?

Jake continued driving. He turned on the narrow road by the tree-filled park that led to the back of the station. The snow-covered ground was beautiful and could be a romantic drive, but after their serious conversation, he thought Emma was a problem for her. Tension filled the air.

"Jake, let me explain. I was only trying to say…"

Crash!

Daria screamed. Their truck skidded across the icy road. Jake straightened and kept control of the vehicle. "What happened?"

"Someone just rammed into us. Daria, hold on. A gray pickup is gaining speed and headed straight for us." Jake swerved and skidded. The man's pickup slid off the road and hit a dumpster.

Daria pulled her weapon from her holster and hopped out into the snow. Her head spun. She held on to the car door. A man barreled from the driver's side and ran across the street toward the park. Jake took off after him. Daria steadied herself and jogged in the same direction.

The frozen undergrowth cracked with their footsteps. Snow fell in chunks from playground equipment and the icy tree limbs, making the chase more of an obstacle course. Jake tackled the man and they rolled in the snow. Thankful no children were around, she continued her chase and caught up with them about the time Jake flipped him over and pinned him down.

Daria tugged the ski cap off the man's head, revealing his face.

She gasped. "You."

"Do you know him?" Jake looked up at her, then back at the guy.

"Yes. Richard Schneider. He's the vacationer I arrested. The one I told you about." She stepped closer to him. "What are you doing here? You could have killed us."

"That was the goal." He sneered.

"Are you retaliating against me, or are you taking orders from someone?" She clenched her fists.

The nerve of this guy.

He snickered. "You have no clue who you're dealing with."

No, I don't.

"Drop your weapons." A raspy, angry voice sounded behind them.

Daria's muscles knotted. She regretfully dropped her weapon in the snow.

I know that voice. Jeffers? Whatever's going on, God, please protect us.

Jake kept a straight face. He dropped his weapon.

Richard jumped to his feet and grinned. "They hired me to help get rid of you. Looks like I've almost completed my job."

Daria turned around. Her jaw dropped. Just as she thought. "Lieutenant Jeffers, what are you doing here? What's going on?"

"You refused to be removed from this case. So, now you'll be killed in the line of duty," Jeffers said.

The look on his face and the weapon pointed at her didn't make sense. Was he there to help her, or had he really hired Richard to eliminate her? Daria couldn't wrap her mind around what was happening.

He tossed Richard a rope. "Tie them up. Can't use cuffs or authorities might link their disappearance to someone on the force."

More police officers appeared in the distance and crept up behind Jeffers. She chewed her lip.

Don't flinch or this might not end well.

Jake looked at her. She lightly nodded.

"Don't try anything," Jeffers said. "You forget I know body language, too."

McDaniel's voice shouted from behind the lieutenant. "Jeffers, drop your weapon."

He ignored McDaniel's orders.

"Don't make us take you down." Cramer lifted his weapon at Jeffers.

Daria blinked. Was she dreaming this nightmare? Jeffers, whom she thought was a faithful boss, had betrayed the department and the trust of the town. Had she been both a pawn and a menace in her lieutenant's illegal scheme? She couldn't believe her eyes, and she couldn't get past the regretful look in his eyes.

McDaniel, Evans, Cramer and Smothers, plus several other cops, stood with their weapons in a ready position pointed at their lieutenant.

"Don't make me say it again, Jeffers," McDaniel said. "Drop your weapon."

He dropped his gun and raised his hands in the air. He turned his focus on Jake. "You were supposed to die in that hotel fire."

Jake's face turned red. His knuckles whitened with his clenched fists. Daria gripped his arm to keep him from punching the lieutenant.

Cramer and Evans ran over and grabbed Jeffers. Cramer scooped the pistol up off the ground. Smothers handcuffed Richard and read him his Miranda rights.

McDaniel stepped up beside Daria and handed her a pair of handcuffs. "You can do the honors. Handcuff Jeffers and read him his Miranda rights. The department has been monitoring him for months."

"Why was I not informed of this situation? You mean my life has been in danger and no one thought to warn me?" Heat rose to Daria's cheeks.

"We have evidence that will put him away for years." McDaniel squared his shoulders and looked her in the eyes. "We've been watching Jeffers since you arrested Richard. His demeaning attitude toward you was unwarranted. We began noticing some inconsistencies in his work ethics, but we couldn't figure out what was going on. Things didn't add up, so we watched and waited. Good thing we were still tracking him, or today could have turned out a lot worse."

"But why not inform me? I thought we were all on the same side." Daria rubbed her temples.

"We are on the same team, but he was on your case too much. Then Jake arrives with information about his sister and the supposedly misfiled complaint of death threats which led to her death. You were too close to Jeffers, and you were feeding him information on your investigation." McDaniels stepped back. "Who do you think alerted your stalker to which hotel you took Jake and Emma to?"

A sense of betrayal washed over Daria. Was she used as a decoy to prove Jeffers a rogue officer? He never seemed the type to betray anyone.

McDaniel pointed to the cuffs in her hand. "Cuff him, unless you want me to. It would save a long court hearing time if we could find that last bit of evidence."

Daria snapped the cuffs closed and shook her head. "What evidence? You have the flash drives."

Cramer and Evans took the lieutenant from Daria and put him in the back of the squad car. A place she figured he'd never been. Anger and confusion fumed within her.

Evans tapped Daria on the shoulder. "For the record, we had suspicions about Jeffers's illegal activity, so we had to play along. And I'm sorry to say part of that playing along meant harassing you about your temper and trying to humiliate you into quitting your job. He knew you were a good cop, and you'd stop at nothing to uncover his wrongdoing if you caught wind of it. You didn't deserve the hazing the department gave you at his orders."

"He was responsible? This boggles my mind. I can't wrap my head around what just happened. What evidence do you have on him?" Daria fought tears at this new revelation.

"We found an unusually large sum of money in his bank account. He insisted it wasn't his, but we both know people don't just drop money in private accounts." Evans let out a huff. "I'd like to believe him, but you know as well as I do that we have to follow protocol. Arresting him is part of it. Besides, he just assaulted you and Jake and was about to eliminate both of you."

"Thank you for clarifying." Daria turned to Jake, who stood beside her. "Now I have a double report to complete, and I'm not sure how to answer all the questions."

He put his arm around her shoulders and walked her back to the truck. Her sore shoulder still ached a little, but not as bad as her concussion.

McDaniel ran toward her. She paused, questioning the serious look on his face.

Something isn't right.

"Daria, I just received word from my confidential informant that this case isn't over. Now that Jeffers is in custody, there's an additional threat stirring. And they're after the rest of the evidence."

Chills raced down her spine. "I still don't know what evidence they mean. And how many people are tied to this crime? I thought we had everyone."

Jake rushed Daria back to the truck, where she'd have a bit of shelter if a shooter was still close by. He slid on the icy road trying to clear the area. Had the person hired a sniper or a stalker? He couldn't take any chances. Daria's safety was of utmost importance.

Daria's nostrils flared. He'd seen that look before. Either she was furious or engulfed in fear. Her fist hit the seat. She was angry.

Jake drove as fast as he could on the slick roads. His tires slipped a few times. He'd get her out of the public eye as soon as possible. The station first, to fill out her report before any detail faded, then to the safety of her brother's home.

She rubbed her forehead.

It had been a while since she'd taken anything for her head. He'd find the medication she needed once they reached their destination. All the movement she'd encountered this morning was not what the doctor ordered.

"Almost there," Jake said. "Need to move quick and get inside."

"In case you've forgotten, I don't move quick right now, but I'll do the best I can." Daria unbuckled her seat belt.

"No worries." Jake's insides went into stealth mode. Get her out of the danger zone, should someone be gunning for her, or for him. "I'll help you."

He rushed to the other side of the truck and helped her steady herself from the fast motion. "Come on. I've got you."

"Let's go to the small conference room where we had breakfast yesterday. I prefer the security it provides." She held her head high. "I'm not going to fall over. It's this relentless throbbing in my head. Makes my stomach queasy."

He walked her inside and sat her in a chair. "Where do I find medicine for your head?"

"Jake, I can get it. I'm not an invalid." She pushed to get up.

He stopped her. "You rest, please. Just tell me where to find it."

"Cramer keeps a bottle of over-the-counter pain reliever on his desk. It's down the hall toward the front of the building. You can't miss it. He likes to fish. You'll see a largemouth bass mounted on the wall of his office."

"Be back in a sec." Jake's pulse worked double time.

He walked at a steady but fast pace. His marine training kicked in. Hostiles could be anywhere, and he trusted no one. Especially since Jeffers was involved. How many other officers had gone rogue?

He passed several cubicles where officers sat working. A mounted fish caught his attention off to the side in an actual office.

Cramer must carry clout to have an office like this.

There on the desk was the large bottle Daria described. He scooped up the bottle.

Jake made a loop around all the cubicles and found a kitchen. He looked around, then stepped inside. The refrigerator held soft drinks and the coffeepot sat half-full. He felt the pot. Barely warm. He slipped a couple of soft drinks into his pockets and picked up two bags of potato chips from a large bowl containing multiple single-size snack bags.

Back in the room, Daria sat with her head in her hands. He placed the bottle of pain relievers on the table in front of her.

"Oh, you found it." She poured two tablets into her palm. "Thank you."

"You're welcome." He tossed the chips on the table, retrieved the canned drinks and popped open both cans. "I raided the kitchen. Coffee was cold."

"Thanks. Something salty looks good right now. Maybe it will help calm my stomach, too." Daria placed the two pills in her mouth and took a drink of her soda. "Jake, I need to finish what I was saying before the crash. I love Emma so very much. I'd love to hold her and steal kisses from her every day. I only thought you might want more one-on-one time with her before I enter the picture."

Jake looked up at her. "Don't you get it? You're already in the picture."

Daria sat back, staring at him. "I didn't look at it in that way." She smiled.

He reached over, put his finger under her chin and planted a brief kiss on her lips. "It's all good." He ripped the chips open and handed her the bag. "Where do I find the papers or the report you need to fill out?"

Daria looked up at him and rolled her eyes. "I should have told you when you went to get meds. I can go."

"Humor me. Let me get what you need. You should be at your brother's house resting." He placed his hand on the doorknob. "Now, tell me what to look for?"

She let out a huff and dropped her shoulders. "Fine. My cubicle is straight across from Cramer's office. Grab my iPad off the top of my desk. That's what I use to complete reports."

"You're right, I could've gotten everything in one fell swoop." He stepped out and closed the door. She was so independent.

I'm the same way, maybe even more so. Determined. The Marine Corps made sure of that.

Her iPad was right where she said it would be. He retrieved it and the power cord.

He spun and turned the corner out of the cubicle. He stopped abruptly. What was that on the floor in Cramer's office? Jake stood tall and checked across the room. No one appeared interested in his presence and no one peeked over the top of their cubicle walls.

He backed up and walked around Cramer's desk. His

heart skipped a beat and heat rose into his face. Two of the rubber flash drive toys lay by one of the wheels of his rolling office chair. A small drawer to the left wasn't shut all the way. He pulled it open with his little finger. The entire collection of Emma's flash drives had been tossed inside.

Jake reasoned that he'd been so focused on the pain reliever bottle he hadn't paid attention to what was on the floor.

Best he could tell, it appeared Cramer must have been in a hurry to leave, so he'd tossed them in, two fell out without him knowing, and he'd failed to close the drawer completely. Was Cramer involved? Why weren't the flash drives in a more secure place?

Jake fumed. He scooped them all up and dropped the two-inch drives in both of his pants pockets, then casually walked back to the small conference room.

Daria's tired eyes searched him as he walked in. "What took so long?"

Jake placed her iPad and cord on the table, then emptied his pockets. The rubber toys toppled onto the table in front of her. "This."

Her jaw dropped. "Jake, where did you get these? They are supposed to be locked away in the evidence room. You can't just take things."

"Cramer's office."

Her eyes widened. Instant tears rolled down her cheeks. "Oh, no. Is he involved, too? He's such a nice guy and a longtime friend. Is he our threat now? Jake, this is too much. Who else is involved?"

"I don't know, but we're getting out of here." Jake

stuffed the toys back into his pockets and took her hand. "Let's go."

She picked up her iPad and shoved the cord in her coat pocket. "Get your soda and chips. We don't want to leave evidence that we were here. I know you've been all over the building, but half the time we don't pay attention to who is walking around. At least, not in our small town, where we rarely have trouble."

"Got it." Jake opened the door and escorted Daria to the truck. He hopped in the driver's seat and eased the truck back onto the town's main street. He wasn't naive enough to believe no one saw them, but he didn't have to make it look like they took off in a hurry, or were guilty, per se.

Daria's straight posture let Jake know her thoughts were reeling in what had just happened and probably theorizing the situation. He had to remain alert and watch for hostiles.

"Thoughts?" Jake considered holding her hand, but he didn't want to overwhelm her.

"Cramer is a 'by the book' type of cop." She was silent for a moment. "Doesn't make sense for him to be so careless or sloppy with valuable evidence. I may be wrong, but my gut tells me someone is trying to set him up."

"Makes sense after seeing the toys scattered like that. We still need to be cautious around him until we know for sure." Jake gave in and squeezed her hand, then let go. "But if someone is setting him up, who could it be? Any idea?"

She rubbed her forehead again. "Not at the moment. I'm thankful the meds are finally kicking in."

"You might process things better if we turned into a drive-through and got something to eat. These chips aren't going to hold us long." His stomach growled.

Daria lifted her eyebrows.

He laughed. "I'm hungry. What do you say?"

"Sure. I wouldn't want a tough marine to go without a meal."

Her playful humor lightened the mood. She felt better.

He drove into the burger joint's parking lot and sat in the drive-through line with other cars. "What would you like?"

"Whatever you're getting."

"Really? Two cheeseburgers with all the fixings, fries and a chocolate milkshake?"

"What?" Her head spun. "No. You must be starving. Just get me the junior burger and fries. I have a soda already."

They placed their order and approached the window for their food. Two cars passed by them and parked side by side. One backed in and one pulled in, aligning the driver's windows. Daria's hand slammed against his arm, almost making him drop his shake.

"Look." She slid down in her seat.

Jake placed his shake in the cup holder. He pressed his head back in the headrest's leather and tried to avoid being seen. Cramer and someone wearing a hat and scarf covering half their face. From the distance, it looked as though Cramer's face reddened. Cramer shook his head "no" and pulled away.

Had either of them spotted Daria and him? The other

car backed out and drove the wrong way out of the parking lot.

Jake reached over to the serving window and got their food. "What was that all about?"

ELEVEN

Daria's stomach twisted, and it wasn't her concussion causing the discomfort. Why had Cramer met with an unidentified person in a busy place? Maybe he thought the busier the better, and no one would notice. If the situation were different, she may not have given him a second look, but there was too much going on. She and Jake had to keep their eyes open.

"I don't know what's going on. I thought Jeffers was calling the shots, but evidently there's someone else picking up where he left off, unless he wasn't the head of the operation." She bit into her burger and stuffed a fry in her mouth.

"We can eat on the way, but I'm thinking we need to have a serious discussion with your brother. Maybe he has some insight or suspicions, so we can formulate a plan." Jake slurped his milkshake.

"I agree." Daria didn't want to think too hard. It increased the pounding in her head, which was more due to stress than concussion at this point. "Let's go find Robert. We have his truck, so we know he's working from home today."

Silence ruled inside the vehicle as they finished their

fast food. The temperature outside had warmed a little, but Gina had mentioned another cold front coming through later in the day with another foot of snow. Daria couldn't control the weather, but maybe, with the help of Jake and Robert, she could figure things out.

She glanced at Jake. Her heart beat faster. Not only was he handsome, but inside that marine-tough exterior, he was still the guy who loved to have fun, and she had fallen in love with him already. She could hardly wait to be free of this deadly case and see where life with him and Emma would lead.

They turned into her brother's driveway. Undisturbed snow always looked like a fluffy blanket until children scurried around the lawn and built a snowman. One arm was a small stick, the other a branch. She couldn't help but chuckle.

"I'm ready to see Emma, then we'll find my brother." Daria picked up her iPad and opened her door before Jake could make it around the truck. Isaac and Alexa ran out of the front door, excited to show off their snow creation. Gina stood at the glass door, holding Emma.

"Look what we did," Alexa said as she jumped up and down and clapped her glove-covered hands.

"It's beautiful." Daria kissed her cheek.

"I helped do most of it." Isaac stuffed his hands in his coat pockets. "She's not very good at building a snowman."

"I am too." Alexa huffed and propped her hands on her waist.

Daria pulled them close and gave them a big hug. "Both of you did a splendid job of making that snowman look real. Just like Frosty."

"We're going to build another one." Isaac took off running, with Alexa trailing behind.

Daria admired both of the kids' enthusiasm. She stepped onto the porch and went inside while Jake held the door open for her. She leaned toward Gina and kissed Emma on the cheek. Warmth inside the house felt like someone had wrapped her in an electric blanket. She sniffed the air. "Is that spiced cider I smell?"

Gina tilted her head and smiled. "Yes. I remembered how you raved about it the last time I made it. Thought you might like some after all you've been through."

"You are so thoughtful."

Jake had already tossed his coat aside and taken Emma into his arms. Such a sweet sight. He kissed Emma's neck, and she giggled. His face brightened as admiration and love for her revealed itself. He fluffed her curls. She ducked from under his hand.

He kissed her neck again and faced Daria. "Sorry, I had to get some Uncle Jake lovin' from my girl."

"Don't let me stop you." Daria slid her coat off and placed it on the coatrack by the door. She picked up Jake's coat and hung it up, too. Seeing this tall, muscular marine cuddling with his dainty niece was a postcard-perfect picture. "She missed you."

Gina returned to the living room with two cups of her homemade spiced cider. Emma kicked her legs to get down. Jake placed her on the floor. She toddled over to the security door and slapped the glass, leaving tiny handprints. She giggled and danced in place, watching Isaac and Alexa playing in the snow.

"Thank you." Daria took the cups and handed Jake one. "The best hot cider anytime of the year, but especially on a wintry day." She sniffed and blew at the steaming beverage. "Smells fabulous." She sipped the drink. "Perfect."

Jake followed suit. He smacked his lips and smiled. "Very good. Thank you."

"You're both welcome." Gina motioned to the sofa. "Have a seat and enjoy or join us in the kitchen. Robert is working on his laptop."

"Oh, good." Daria motioned to Jake, who had already relaxed in the living room. "We needed to discuss some business stuff with him. Some crazy things are happening, and we're hoping he can give us insight or direction."

"Well, go right in." Gina wiped her hands on a paper towel. "I need to fold clothes, and I'll let Emma help me. She loves to empty the basket and fill it back up."

"Thank you, again, Gina. You are so thoughtful." Daria walked into the kitchen. "Good afternoon. What are you focused on?" She set her cup on the table and pulled out a chair.

"Hey, man, hope we're not interrupting." Jake sat in the chair beside her.

Robert closed his laptop, leaned back in his chair and took a drink from his cup. "How are you feeling today after that nasty concussion?"

"The headache has been on and off. Jake has kept me on a pain reliever schedule." She patted Jake's arm. "The department has a problem. I don't know if you've heard about it yet."

Robert's eyebrows lowered and wrinkles appeared on his forehead. "Um, no. I've been working on an Excel spreadsheet all day." He sat up straight. "What's up?"

"First off," Daria said. "Did you know that Lieutenant Jeffers was under surveillance?"

Robert wiped his hand across his mouth. "Why do you ask?"

"Because they arrested him today after holding Jake and me at gunpoint. McDaniel, Evans, Cramer and Smothers, plus a handful of other cops, came up from behind and arrested him. That young vacationer, Richard Schneider, that I arrested a while back was involved with Jeffers. He's in custody, too." Daria opened her iPad. "What can you tell me? Obviously, you know something or your reaction to my question would have been different."

"I'm an investigator with the department, Daria, and there are some things I am not at liberty to share, even with family." Robert sat back and crossed one leg over the other. "I knew there were suspicions of his hands being dirty, but we hadn't gathered enough evidence to make an arrest."

"You could've warned me or told me to watch my back or something." Daria closed her eyes and took in a deep breath. "I worked with him every day. He could have killed me at any time. Honestly, I still can't bring myself to believe he is guilty." She couldn't blame her brother for doing his job. If only she'd had an inkling that Jeffers may have gone rogue.

Jake spoke up. "Kind of like the old saying of being between a rock and a hard place. I've been in those situations while on active duty. Not necessarily by my peers or my comrades, but in some tough places. I get it."

"Now that we know you know about the behind-the-scenes stuff," Daria continued, "Jake found those toy flash drives in Cramer's office."

Robert dropped his leg and sat up again. "Cramer? What does he have to do with the case?"

"You tell us." Daria stood and walked to the kitchen window.

"We returned to the station after someone rammed your truck from behind and the whole takedown took place." Jake scooted to the edge of his seat.

"Wait, somebody hit my truck?" Robert jumped to his feet. "How bad is it, and why were you in Cramer's office?"

"Sorry, but yes. The damage isn't too bad. Just a dent in the fender. I went to Cramer's office and got Daria his bottle of over-the-counter pain meds." Jake continued explaining how things went and how he found the toy flash drives.

"Cramer isn't that sloppy. He'd never remove incriminating evidence and toss it around carelessly. Sounds like a setup." Robert plopped down in his chair and crossed his arms.

"That's what we thought. Maybe even Jeffers." Daria chewed on her lip. "On top of that, we pulled through the town's burger joint, and while we were waiting in line at the drive-through, who do you think we spotted?" She went through the whole scenario with Cramer and an unidentified person.

"We eased away, unnoticed, I hope." Jake gulped his drink.

Robert tapped a finger on his lips. "Cramer has an impeccable record. He's by far one of the best cops we've had in years, outside of you, sister." He winked at her.

Daria shook her head. "Don't go there. I know I've

messed up plenty of times. You're right, Cramer is trust-worthy and an outstanding officer."

"Any idea who the person in the other car was? Male? Female?" Robert asked.

"They made great efforts to conceal their identity." Jake walked over to the stove where the pot of hot cider sat. "Mind if I have another cup?"

"Help yourself." Gina walked in with a stack of kitchen towels and put them in a drawer. "If you need anything, just give me a shout. I'll be in the other room."

Emma toddled behind her. "Ma, ma, ma, ma." Her eyes lit up when she saw Jake. She ran to him with her arms lifted, holding her rubber giraffe.

"She's gotten comfortable with you." Daria reached over and smoothed her fingers across the top of Emma's soft hand. She pulled her chair out and sat back down.

Emma straightened her legs and wanted down again. Jake let her slide off his lap. She went back into the living room with Gina.

"Anything else?" Robert's eyes shifted from Daria to Jake, then back to Daria.

Jake cleared his throat.

"Yes. One minor detail." Daria paused. "McDaniel said a trusted source heard we are still in danger because evidently there is a missing piece of evidence this unknown person wants." She lifted her hands and dropped them to her lap. "What are we overlooking, Robert? Any clue what evidence they want?"

Jake stood and paced. What he thought would be a quiet return to civilization had turned into another fight for his life that involved two innocents. He'd never known his old hometown to have this much mystery behind it.

Daria's cell rang. He spun and faced her. Her phone hadn't rung in two days.

"Hello?" Her eyes went from him to her brother, then back to him. "No way." Her hand covered her eyes and her voice cracked. "How did it happen? Okay. Thanks for calling." She sat staring at her cup.

"Spit it out, Daria." Robert leaned forward.

Jake returned to his seat and took her hand. "What happened?"

"Smothers was just found dead in his car a few minutes ago." Daria covered her face with both hands. "Gunshot to the head."

Heat rushed to Jake's face. He clenched his fists. "This has gotten out of hand. We've got to stop this senseless violence before someone else dies."

If he could encourage Daria to rest, he could slip away and do some investigating. He stood and put his hands on both of her shoulders, remembering one was still sore. "This has been an unusually long, stressful day. Why don't you go rest a little while?"

She spun and glared up at him. "Jake Fisher, I know what you're thinking, and you aren't going scouting without me."

Jake dropped his jaw.

Busted.

Robert pushed to his feet. "And neither of you are going anywhere without me. Besides, it's my truck."

"You've got a point there." Jake shoved his hands into his pockets and shrugged. "That settles it. Where do we begin?"

They all marched into the living room and grabbed their coats. Robert tossed Jake a pair of gloves. Jake helped Daria with her coat. She borrowed a scarf from Gina's coatrack and wrapped it around her neck.

"Weapons?" Robert asked as he checked his and clipped it to his waistband.

Jake lifted his jacket, shirt and all, exposing his shoulder holster. "Got mine."

Daria patted her side. "Mine, too."

Gina stood with her hands propped at her waist. "Do I need one, too?"

Jake watched as Robert walked over and kissed his wife. "You know where yours is if you need it. Someone killed Smothers. We've got to go."

"Oh, dear, that poor man." Gina covered her mouth, then leaned over and picked up Emma, who rubbed her eyes. "Let me know if I can do anything. Please be careful."

The worried look on Gina's face tugged at Jake's heart. This family, this town, shouldn't be going through such a dangerous time. It was almost Christmas. Everyone should be happy. He had to help them get this beautiful tourist town safe again.

Robert's kids ran circles out in the front yard, throwing snowballs at each other. A flash of Amanda and him, throwing snowballs as kids, then tackling their snowman and knocking him over, swirled through his memory. The pain of loss pierced his heart. His brave sister, Amanda, exposed this huge crime.

Jake hopped in the passenger side of the king cab truck beside Daria, with Robert at the wheel. He enjoyed sitting close to her, but he would have liked it better if she had stayed at the house with Gina and the kids.

"You could've gotten in the back, Daria. You would have had a lot more room." Robert backed out of the driveway and pulled out onto the road.

"Are you kidding? I'm right between you two men. Now I'll hear every detail of your conversations," she said.

Jake took her hand in his. He cared for her deeply. She had clarified her comment about Emma. He loved her and knew she loved Emma. Thoughts of moving forward with their relationship felt right.

"Don't you two get serious about each other and think you're going to hang around all the time." Robert grinned. He reached the end of the road and pulled out onto the main highway.

"We make a great team." Jake squeezed her hand. "What's the plan, and where do we begin at four in the afternoon?"

"I figure we should get to the station before shift change and question everyone there. Then, question the second shift personnel as they clock in. After that, we will walk the streets and question town citizens without alarming the tourists. Somebody knows something," Robert said.

"Exactly," Jake chimed in. They were going to be great friends. Robert and he thought alike. He might even become his brother-in-law one day if it worked out with Daria.

Jake's insides jumped backflips. Finally, they were doing the chasing instead of the running and hiding. His type of tactics. There'd been so much uncertainty earlier, he didn't want to put Daria in harm's way. Maybe he'd been too overprotective. She was a cop. Injured or not, she was determined to see the case through. He couldn't blame her.

"Whoever is looking for us will be surprised with us out in public asking questions," Daria said. "May even force them into making a move."

"It's a risk we have to take, like bombarding the enemy lines." Jake placed his arm on the door's armrest. "A risk we have to take if we want to conquer the enemy."

They arrived at the station and went inside. Robert stood at the front desk and announced that no one was to leave until each person answered a few questions.

Jake enjoyed the interviews and studied each person's body language. Everyone took part even though they grieved the loss of Smothers and the shocking news of Jeffers's arrest. After all the officers from the day shift had been questioned, Jake roamed the department to see if they'd missed anyone.

Daria caught up with him in the kitchen and got a bottled water from the refrigerator. Jake poured himself a cup of fresh coffee.

"This shift was in the clear. Now we wait for the next." He lifted his cup to his lips. "That's hot."

Daria backed up and stared at him.

"What?" Jake took another sip.

"You realize this is where I work. You don't. You're a civilian and you're sure making yourself at home." A grin slid across her face.

"Of course, but my girl and her brother work here, so I figure it gives me a little clout." He moved to the kitchen doorway. "Looks like shift change to me."

"You are impossible." Daria worked her way around him. "Maybe you should get a job here."

Jake caught up with her. "You know, that's not a bad idea. I'll think about it." He looked across the room at the officers coming and going. He wouldn't mind working here. He figured since he was physically fit, a sharp-shooter, had experience reading body language and all those other things an officer should be able to accomplish, he'd fit the position.

Another round of questioning went as well as could be expected once word spread of their fallen officer and the possible betrayal of their lieutenant. Only one person remembered seeing Jeffers rush into Cramer's office earlier in the day, which could explain the unethical placement of the toy flash drives. But no one knew anything about additional evidence.

Jake followed Daria and Robert to the front of the station. He stared across the street to all the patrons walking the sidewalks and going in and out of souvenir shops. Christmas tinsel and fake snow decorated shop windows. One shop even had a small flashing train circling a miniature decorated tree.

The snow made the town look even more festive, but it meant they had a cold investigative outing ahead of them.

"Jake. Are you listening?"

Daria's voice brought him back from admiring the town. "What? Yep."

"What did we just say?"

Busted again.

Daria reached up and turned his head in her direction. "You and I will stroll along casually and talk to people. Robert will do his own window shopping and see what he can find out."

"Sounds like a plan to me." Jake took Daria's hand. "Which side do you prefer walking on so you can get to your gun if needed?"

"Switch sides." Daria held her hand out. "Robert, are you ready?"

Robert turned his coat collar up and stuck his hands in his pockets. "Ready."

Jake paused. "Wait. Where do we want to meet up and what time?"

"It's 8:00 p.m. now. Let's meet at the Oakland Grill at 10:00 p.m. By then we'll be icicles and ready for something hot to drink."

"I agree." Jake rolled his neck until it popped. Adrenaline had his body feeling like a jet revving up to get going. "Let's go."

He and Daria held hands and strolled up the town's main street, greeting passersby. It dawned on Jake that he couldn't tell tourists from townspeople. He leaned closer to Daria's ear.

"I have to go with your lead. I don't know who is vacationing and who lives here. Everyone looks the same. I'm probably the one who sticks out like a drop of strawberry ice cream in a bowl of vanilla."

She laughed. "No worries. I'll introduce you to the locals as long as I can remember their names."

Jake shivered with a gust of wind. The temperatures had dropped since they'd arrived earlier. Small snowflakes peppered down. Light Christmas music filtered down the street and shoppers were dressed in their winter coats and hats. No one had a clue there was a killer on the loose.

TWELVE

Daria squeezed Jake's hand every time they met a local. Most of them were harmless, out doing their Christmas shopping. A few homeless people hung around a fire in a fifty-five-gallon drum at the entrance of an alley at the north end of town.

"Who would be crazy enough to stalk someone in this freezing weather?" Jake wrapped his arm around Daria's shoulders.

She leaned her head toward him. "An actual stalker or criminal watching for the right moment to strike. You should know that, Mr. Marine. Let's talk to these guys."

Some men moved away as she approached. She'd seen them before, and they knew she was a cop.

Jake tossed a hand up. "Hey, guys, hope you're staying warm by that fire."

A couple of them grumbled.

"Good evening," Daria said. "How's everyone hanging tonight? Hey, Monti, Greg, Trevor, and is that Randall over there? We're not here to bother you guys. It's much too cold. Did any of you hear about Officer Smothers being shot today?"

"Nope. Too bad, though. I liked the guy." Trevor held

his hands over the fire. His fingerless gloves didn't do much to keep his hands warm.

"Yeah, I heard." Randall stepped out of the shadows. "Makes us kinda nervous. We don't know who done it."

"Who would kill a cop in our quiet town?" Monti coughed and spat in the fire.

"I don't know, guys, but if you hear anything, would you let me know? We want to make sure everyone stays safe and has a nice Christmas." Daria stepped back. "Stay warm."

Jake lightly bumped against her shoulder. "You handled that like a pro."

"Thanks. I've had a little experience, and most of those men know me." Her foot slipped on an icy patch, and Jake caught her before she hit the ground.

"That was close." He helped her stand upright but held her next to him.

Her heart fluttered with expectation.

Jake glanced around, then back at her. "Since Jeffers isn't here and you're not specifically on duty, may I have permission to kiss you?"

"A quick kiss. I don't want to draw too much attention." She prepared herself. Anticipation increased.

He settled her on her feet, took her into his arms and planted a kiss on her lips. He moved back slowly and smoothed the back of his hand across her cheek.

"Was that quick enough?" He grinned.

Warmth rose to her cheeks. Had her face turned red? "That wasn't quick and unnoticeable, but it was really nice."

"Want me to try again?" Jake's childish grin made her laugh.

"Maybe later." Daria straightened her coat and shivered. "The Oakland Grill is down the street, three blocks away. I don't know about you, but my feet and hands are almost frozen, and the snowflakes are getting bigger. I'm sure Robert is already there warming up and drinking coffee."

She tried not to show her ecstatic feelings as she held her hand out to him. He didn't hesitate. His big, gloved hand wrapped around hers. "Let's go find your brother."

Shoppers dwindled, and the once-crowded walkways grew scarce. Even the locals knew when to call it a night. Jake was right again. The likelihood of locating anyone who knew anything about Smothers's death in the freezing temperatures was zilch to none.

They trekked down the street at a decent pace, watching for ice along the way. Mostly snow crunched under their feet. A few more steps past the alley and they'd be in the restaurant's warmth.

"Psst."

Daria stopped and looked across the street.

"What are you doing?" Jake asked.

"I heard something."

"Psst."

She spun and faced the alley, surprised to see Mr. Treadway, her elderly friend who helped at the restaurant. He stood in the shadows of the streetlight. She dropped Jake's hand and entered the alley, noting Jake towering over her. He was in protection mode, and she appreciated it. Not that she didn't trust Mr. Treadway, but she didn't trust the killers wouldn't see him talking to her and threaten him.

"Mr. Treadway, what are you doing out here without

your coat? May I help you back inside?" Daria touched his thin arm.

"Shhhh." He put a bony finger to his lips. "I wanted to talk to you, but you were busy. I heard somebody talking on their cell about some kind of toy flash drives you found. He stood right by the kitchen door within earshot of me. Said that information was useless to the police unless they found the little black codebook that had all the names in it." He shivered. "I gotta get back inside but figured that's what you and your brother were looking for. Mind you, don't tell nobody you talked to me. I'm just an old man minding my business." He turned and hobbled to the side door of the restaurant.

"You're amazing, Mr. Treadway. Did you get a look at the person?"

"Nope. And I couldn't tell if it was a man or a woman. The voice was muffled. But I'm guessing a man." He stepped inside and closed the door.

Jake opened the main entrance door for her to enter the restaurant. "There had to be at least two of them talking."

"That's true. And that still means at least two more people are involved." Daria pulled off her gloves. "There's Robert at that back table. He has a thing about sitting with his back to the wall."

"I get it." Jake walked behind her and pulled her chair out when they reached the table. No sooner had they sat down than the server walked up for their order.

"I'll have hot tea." She picked up a menu. "Hot vegetable soup with cornbread sounds good, too."

"Coffee, black." Jake took his coat off and hung it over the back of his chair. "I need to look at the menu."

Robert cupped his hands around his coffee mug. "No leads on my end of the street. What about the two of you?"

The server returned to the table with their hot beverages and took Jake's order.

Jake leaned close to the table. "I'll let Daria tell you what she found out."

Daria looked around to make sure no one was listening. "You know Mr. Treadway, right?"

"Yes. He works here in the kitchen," Robert said. "An older gentleman."

"Right." Daria leaned toward her brother. "He stopped us in the alley right beside the restaurant." She explained what she'd learned. "Bless his heart. He's as good as they come."

"Where do we find this so-called black codebook? Any hints?" Robert leaned back for the server to place his food on the table. "Before you ask. I ordered about five minutes before you got here."

"Couldn't wait, I see." She snickered. "He didn't say."

Jake drummed his fingers on the table, then stopped. "We've searched my sister's house once already. Guess we could go back and search again now that we have more details."

"Question is—" she eyed them both. "—do we want to wait until morning or go tonight?"

"We've all had a busy day," Robert said. "Let's get some rest and start fresh tomorrow."

"Agreed." Daria's nerves were on edge. Her shoulder ached a little and her head hurt. Another one of Jake's kisses might make the hurt go away. The thought warmed her heart. Maybe before they turned in for the night.

After the late-night meal, they grew silent on the drive home.

The living room lights were still on in Robert's house. Gina must have left them on for their return. Fresh snow glistened under the one streetlight her brother had installed on their property. Tire tracks streaked the driveway, and two sets of footprints trekked to the front porch. Someone must have visited Gina while they were away.

Robert pulled into the driveway. "Something's not right. We weren't expecting company."

Jake shot out of the truck before Robert came to a full stop. Daria scooted to the edge of the seat and waited for her brother to park. They both hopped out and ran to the front door but it was locked. Jake pulled his weapon and pointed to footprints in the snow that led to the window.

Robert and Daria did likewise. This wasn't good. Not good at all. Adrenaline shot through her body like a triple shot of caffeine. One of the front windows had been knocked out.

Robert pushed past both of them with his weapon in a ready position. Jake shook his head and did hand signals to say he'd go through the window first. Robert wanted to go first. Daria was the cop. She should go first. But it was Robert's home. He unlocked the front door and eased inside with Jake and her close behind. The house was quiet.

Robert and Jake eased up the stairs. Daria checked the dining room and sunroom. Nothing. She eased into the kitchen and her heart plummeted. Gina was tied to a chair. Her head was slumped over and trickles of blood dripped on her blouse.

She checked Gina's pulse. It was steady. She couldn't yell at the guys until she knew the house was clear of the intruders. She untied her about the time Robert and Jake entered. Robert rushed over to her and patted her cheeks.

"Gina, Gina, wake up. Talk to me." He smoothed her hair back from her face. "Honey, what happened?"

Daria called 911.

Gina moaned and opened her eyes. Tears exploded. "They took Emma."

"No." Jake's hands grabbed his head. "This can't be happening." He paced in the kitchen, then stopped, took in a deep breath and studied the scene before him. Hostiles had invaded their safe zone, and it was up to him to track them down.

Robert had to care for his family, and Daria wasn't at full capacity. Sirens grew closer and flashing lights lit up the night. Isaac and Alexa hopped down the stairs, rubbing their eyes. Robert met them in the living room and explained their mom had a bump on the head. The paramedics were going to make sure she was okay.

"Did Mama's visitors do that to her?" Alexa asked.

Jake kneeled in front of her. "Who were your mom's guests?"

"We never saw them before," Isaac said. "Mom told us to go back to bed and shut our doors. She was rocking Emma, and the people wanted to talk."

Daria squatted beside Jake.

"Yeah, I wanted a drink, but Mama said she'd bring it to me when the people left." Alexa leaned against Daria. "I was really thirsty."

"I'll get you a drink." Daria eased into the kitchen, which was now filled with paramedics and cops. She was back in the living room in an instant.

Jake needed to be in the kitchen to hear Gina's story, but he needed to hear what these kids were telling him.

"Want me to take care of the kids while you go in the kitchen?" Daria pulled Alexa close and handed her the water.

How did she know his thoughts? "Yes, thanks." Jake bolted into the kitchen just as the paramedic was finishing assessing Gina and one of the officers came over to take her statement.

"Blood pressure is normal… But she can go ahead with the statement now," the paramedic said.

Gina turned to the officer. "There was a knock at the front door. The porch light wouldn't come on. Before I knew it, glass shattered. Two men busted the window and jumped inside with guns." Gina wiped tears while the paramedic bandaged her head. "It happened so fast I didn't get a good look at them. Emma was asleep in my arms, and Alexa and Isaac crept down the stairs, but I told them to go back up. One man jerked Emma away and wrapped her in the blanket from my couch. I fought with them and that's the last thing I remember."

Jake's inside boiled. His heart hurt.

"The cut on your head is superficial, but since you lost consciousness for an unknown period, we need to transport you to the hospital." The paramedic packed his supplies in his bag.

"No. I'm not leaving my family tonight." Gina grabbed Robert's hand. "I'll go see my doctor tomorrow."

Jake returned to the living room, where the kids sat on the sofa with Daria.

She looked up at him, then back at the kids. "Why don't you guys run upstairs and play or go back to sleep? I need to talk to Jake."

"I want to stay with my mom." Isaac moved closer to the kitchen.

"Is Emma coming back? Did that bad man hurt her?" Alexa asked.

Jake swallowed the lump in his throat. He placed his hand gently on Isaac's back. "Your mom is going to be okay. Your dad and the paramedics are here taking care of her." Then he turned to Alexa. "Emma is okay, too. No one's going to hurt her. Everything is under control and you guys are safe. Go give your mom a hug and you can go play."

After the kids wrapped their arms around their mom, they trudged up the stairs to their rooms, and Jake waited to hear what Daria had found out from them. Nervous energy wouldn't let him sit.

"Anything?" Jake shuffled his feet.

"According to Alexa, it was a man and a woman dressed up like a man. The description of the woman suspiciously sounds like the woman from the restaurant who told us about the flash drives." Daria's hand gripped his arm. "I never suspected her."

"What about the man?" Jake asked.

"The guy was about as tall as her daddy, but Alexa said he was skinny like Isaac. By that description, I assume he is tall and lanky."

"I'm going to my house to look for the book." Jake zipped his coat. He'd never taken it off when they entered the house. "They'll hold Emma hostage until they get what they want."

"I'll go with you." Daria headed toward the door.

"No. It's best I go alone." Jake went in the kitchen and got the truck keys from Robert. He walked past Daria, who still stood at the door. "I'll find Emma. You need to take care of your family."

Jake got in the truck and started backing around all the emergency vehicles. Daria came running out of the house holding Emma's diaper bag and coat. She ran to the passenger side. He unlocked the door and she hopped inside.

"What are you doing?" Jake's emotions were all over the place.

"I'm taking care of my family, like you said. I'm coming with you." She buckled up. "When we find Emma, she's going to want her sippy cup and giraffe."

He spun the tires, trying to move too fast. His baby was in danger, and the woman he loved had been attacked too many times already. How was he supposed to process those emotions?

"Jake, I understand the anxiety right now." Daria shifted in her seat and faced him. "We will find her. I love Emma and I love you."

His insides calmed a bit, but not the distress over Emma's abduction. He reached over and took her hand.

She placed her other hand on top of his. "You and Emma *are* my life."

"Then let's go find our baby." Jake put both hands on the steering wheel.

With little to no traffic at midnight, he made it through town faster than he'd expected. He turned into his driveway. Crime scene tape was still draped across the property. The newly installed windows still had the stickers on the glass. He parked and walked to the front door with Daria at his heels, carrying the diaper bag.

"No telling what the inside looks like." He opened the door and flipped on the light. "Not bad. Looks like it did when we left it the other day, after searching for the last piece of evidence."

"Brr. May want to turn the heat on." Daria tossed the diaper bag on the sofa. It turned over and fell to the floor with a thump.

"Was that her sippy cup that hit the floor? Sounded heavy." Jake turned the thermostat on and approached Daria.

She sat on the sofa, picked the bag up and emptied the contents. A few diapers, one sippy cup, wipes, bib, a change of clothes and her cheese bites. "Nothing heavy here." She checked all the pockets and side zipper, then dropped the bag on the floor again.

The same thud sounded.

Jake's curiosity piqued. He joined her on the sofa.

"Okay, there's something here." She stuck her hand down into the diaper bag.

"Let me see." He felt around, then knocked on the bottom with his knuckles. "You're right. There's something there." He turned the cloth of the diaper bag inside out. The bottom had either ripped, or someone had cut it and hand-stitched it closed. His eyes met with Daria's. "Could it be?"

"Rip it open." Daria scooted closer. "She disguised the flash drives. Who knows?"

Jake ripped the hand-stitched seam. A little black

book came into view. He pulled it out and flipped through it. Sure enough, the book contained a list of codes that belonged to a list of names. Addresses, phone numbers, locations, bank account numbers, etc.

"We've had it with us all along." She blew out a long breath.

Jake pulled her into a hug and placed a quick kiss on her lips. "We found it. The evidence needed to put these guys away and the book those two will kill for."

Daria's phone beeped. She looked up at Jake. "Who'd text me at this hour?" She unzipped her coat and retrieved her cell from her shirt pocket. A blocked ID message arrived.

Meet before sunrise at the old dairy barn outside town and bring the book or else your little darling will freeze to death.

Jake jumped to his feet and squeezed his fists. "If they harm Emma, I will, I will… I'm not telling you what I'll do."

"You don't have to, Jake." Daria stood holding the book. "It will all work out. We will find her."

"Do you know where that barn is? I remember one being around here, but I don't know where it's located."

"I've been by there several times, cruising around in my squad car. I'll text back, 'Which building? There are three.'"

Jake sat beside her, watching for a response to her message. He clasped her hand in his. He wasn't alone. Daria had his back, and he had hers.

Her cell beeped again. She held it out for him to see.

The middle one. Time's wasting. No cops.

Daria shook her head. "No cops? Really? I am a cop and they're texting me."

"How long will it take us to get there?" Jake looked at his watch. "Sunrise is at 5:35 a.m. It's 1:15 a.m. now."

"About an hour. I'm calling Robert," Daria said. "Someone needs to know where we're going." She put the call on speaker and held the phone between her and Jake.

"Robert, we found the book," Daria said.

"Thank goodness. Do you have Emma? Have they made contact?" An urgency increased in Robert's voice.

"No, we don't have her yet. They sent a message to meet them at the old dairy farm before sunrise and specified no police."

"You have about four hours. The police are still here. I'll inform them and they can assist."

"No. Don't send anyone." Jake paced while she talked on the phone. His body tensed. "This meeting must go exactly as instructed. Emma's life depends on it."

McDaniel got on the phone. "Jake, we understand this is a deadly situation. We are just as concerned about little Emma as you are, and we won't do anything to compromise the situation."

"Better not, or I'll hold you personally accountable." Jake wiped his mouth with his hand. He'd handled all kinds of enemy tactics during the war and had always pushed his fears aside. Could he pull himself together enough to do the same for Emma?

Daria hung up the phone. "We need to get going so we can be there before sunrise. We can sit and wait until we need to make a move. I wouldn't think they'd harm a baby, but we can't take any chances."

Jake pulled her into a hug and squeezed. "I never thought I'd need help from anyone, but your support right now means the world to me." He released her, took the book and held it in the air. "Let's go get Emma."

God, keep Emma safe. Give us wisdom and the right tactical maneuvers so no one has to die.

THIRTEEN

Even though she was an experienced cop, Daria's stomach still churned. She'd never faced such an intense and dangerous case. Her nerves formed knots in her neck muscles. They were coming down to the wire in this investigation. The next few hours would determine the outcome.

God, I haven't talked to You much, but I know You're here. We need Your protection for Emma and for us as we step into the battle. Right now, we don't have a plan, but I know You do. I'm trusting You to help us end these threats.

"You're quiet." Jake drove the narrow road toward the old dairy farm.

"Figured we could use some prayer about now." Daria chewed her lip. Her hand slid to her weapon. *Still there.*

"I prayed, too." Jake inhaled a deep breath and blew it out. "I'm not good at it, but if you prayed, maybe God heard one of us."

"Jake, God hears all prayers, including yours and mine. Prayers don't have to be perfect." Daria stared at the snow glistening from the truck's headlights.

Was Emma warm? Were they so inhumane as to let her freeze? Did they hurt her?

Ugh! I can't think like that. God is in control. She had to believe God would answer her prayers.

"How much farther?" Jake swerved around a fallen tree.

"About five miles ahead." She checked her side mirror for signs of squad cars trailing behind. No headlights in sight. If McDaniel, Cramer and Evans were closing in, they would approach without being seen.

"I know you said the woman could be the one from the restaurant." He slowed over a small icy bridge. "But any idea of the man's identity?"

"I've been trying to figure it out. First off, why would the woman tell us about the flash drives, then try to kill us? Where would that have left her? If she'd remained quiet, no telling how long it would have been before we discovered the value of Emma's toys."

"Could she have been fishing for more information, thinking we'd tell her about the book?" He slowed the vehicle down. "Then she'd know for sure we had found it."

"It's possible. She seems to be the one calling the shots. The man is a puzzle to me. Maybe he's related, someone she works with or someone she hired."

Jake pointed. "Is that it ahead?"

"Yes. See the three buildings? You'll turn on the second entrance and follow the dirt, well, icy drive all the way around to the back." Daria leaned toward the window and squinted into the dark. She glanced at her watch. "It's 2:50 a.m. There's no sign of backup."

"Good. It's still early, though. Maybe they listened and will stay away, considering the sensitivity of the situation." Jake turned on the snow-covered driveway. "I remember this place. It's been so long I'd forgotten about it."

"Pull over by that rolled hay bale and park. If we sit in the dark long enough, our eyes might have time to adjust." Daria leaned back in the seat. "If the moon was out, all this snow would make it almost daylight." The silence grew eerie. She studied their surroundings as best as she could. They didn't need anyone sneaking up to the window and blasting them.

Time crept. Tension mounted by the hour as they sat there watching and listening. An ache eased into her head. Should have brought the medication, but no time to think about that now.

"Movement to the right of the building." Jake pointed and whispered so low she almost didn't understand what he'd said.

Daria watched as someone or something slowly distanced itself from the building. "That can't be him or her stepping out from hiding. Oh, it's a buck." She exhaled. "It's going into the woods. We'll give the abductors a few more minutes to make a move. If not, then we'll ease inside the barn."

"I've had to wait hours for the enemy to show their faces," Jake whispered. "Knowing we only have minutes before our encounter only increases the tension. We can do this. I've got confidence in you and your skills."

She reached over and squeezed his forearm. "And I have full confidence in your expert marine tactics."

"Wait. What's that?" Jake pointed toward the barn again.

"It's our cue to get out. Someone stepped to the opening and backed up." She reached for the door handle. "Just remember, you and Emma are going to be okay."

"Don't go saying stuff like that." Jake unbuckled his seat belt and opened his door. "We're both bringing Emma home."

Daria took the book from Jake and stuck it in her coat pocket before she stepped out of the truck and pulled her weapon. Jake held his pistol by his side. He remained by her as they walked toward the old barn. Snow crunched beneath their feet and the frigid wind cut through her clothes, sending chills over her body.

Emma. Where are you, baby?

Neither breathed a word as they approached the entrance and stepped inside the barn. Jake slid to the left, while Daria stepped to the right and moved forward. A flashlight popped on and blinded her. She threw her hand up and covered her eyes like a visor.

"You can stop right there," the scratchy female voice said. "Where's your friend?"

"Why would I answer any of your questions? You're the one in control here. You should know if I came alone or if someone came with me."

"Pretty sure of yourself, aren't you? Well, you can quit with the cocky attitude." Her tone grew angry. "I know Jake is here. If he values that baby's life, he'll show himself." She grew quiet, like she was waiting for Jake to appear.

A rustling sound came from the woman's left, which was Daria's right. Jake had gone the opposite direction. Whoever moved around must be this woman's partner. She scrolled the light around quickly. "That you, T?"

"Yep," a husky voice replied.

Daria took advantage of the second of darkness and jumped behind a hay bale. Jake was in his element and had most likely strategically placed himself out of sight of the woman's flashlight.

"Don't try playing games with me. I can shoot through that hay, Officer Gordon. Toss your weapon or I'll shoot."

"You toss your weapon so we can talk face-to-face." Daria could have already fired at her, but she wanted to gather more information. Like where Emma was.

More rustling grew closer to the front of the barn. Daria squinted to see in the dark. Was it Jake or that man the woman called T? Her senses were on high alert.

"Give me the book and I'll give Emma back." Frustration rose in the woman's voice.

"Not until you drop your gun." Daria rolled against the wood fence. She spotted the dark shadow standing a short distance away.

"Jake, I know you're here. On the count of three, I'm going to shoot your cop friend. One, two, three."

Thump.

Thump.

Thump.

The woman shot into the hay bale three times. Daria pointed her weapon through a crack between the hay and the fence and pulled the trigger. The woman screamed and dropped her flashlight. Daria had aimed knee level in the darkness and wasn't sure she'd hit her target.

Silence.

If she'd hit the woman, it wouldn't have been a deadly shot. More movement, closer to her right, increased the already racing beat of her heart. T must have stepped her direction.

Light filtered over the horizon, through cracks in the wooden walls and into the barn's entrance. They were in for a standoff, for sure. Emma must not be close because there had been no cries of a baby nearby. Where had they left her?

I refuse to believe they were cruel enough to leave her out in these freezing temperatures.

"Come on out, Officer," a deep male voice demanded. "Your time is up. Apparently, your friend left you here to fend for yourself."

"I'll come out if you tell me where you're holding Emma." Daria waited.

"No. Show us the book first." The woman grunted, then laughed. "You barely scraped my leg. Thought you were a sharpshooter."

"If I'd wanted to kill you, you wouldn't be talking to me right now." Daria put her hands in the air, trusting Jake was in his strategy mode. "I'm standing up."

"Toss your weapon toward us and come on out."

The man's familiar voice had her stumped. She'd heard it somewhere but couldn't place it.

I know better than to give up my weapon. But I have to, for Emma's sake. Jake, I'm trusting you.

The thought scrolled through her mind like a stuck recording. She hated to succumb to the woman's demands, but she was at a point of no return until Jake made his move. She tossed it toward them as instructed and stood.

The sun peeked higher over the horizon just enough for Daria to see the same woman she'd seen in the restaurant and "T" the man who stood by her. The sunglasses and scarf still hid her identity. She studied the man. Where had she seen him?

"Trying to figure it all out, aren't you, Officer?" He huffed.

"Guess I am." Daria pointed to the woman. "You said your name was Liz Colton and you worked with Amanda, right?"

"Sort of. Things aren't as they seem, my dear. Amanda worked for my husband. She stole his files. I told him not to use his office computer, but he was all about Excel spreadsheets." She removed her sunglasses and unwrapped the covering from her head.

Daria recognized her right off. She fumed for not demanding the woman to show her face when they met at the restaurant.

Caroline, the banker's wife. A fine respectable lady, or so I thought.

Caroline blew on her fingernail and repositioned her weapon. "I suppose you've figured out that I'm the brains behind this embezzlement scheme, and I don't mind owning up to it. I worked hard to formulate the perfect retirement plan. But that Amanda girl stuck her nose in the wrong place, and it cost her life and the life of her husband. So sad." Her laugh held no remorse.

"Is he your hired help, because I know he's not your husband." Daria sized the man up.

"Shut your mouth and hand over the book." He shoved his gun toward her. The way he held his weapon told Daria he was not an experienced shooter.

"Where's Emma?" Heat rose in Daria's cheeks. This back-and-forth had her blood boiling.

"The book," Caroline demanded. "Tony, get it from her. I'll cover you."

Tony? Tony Schneider? Wasn't that the father's name of that kid she'd arrested? He stuck his weapon in his waistband and walked toward her.

Daria spotted movement back behind Caroline. Either Jake or one of the cops was about to intervene. Despite telling them not to interfere, she wouldn't be surprised if they showed up anyway. They would have entered from an alternate direction. The closer Tony got to her, the more she prepared herself to tackle him and prayed it was the right move.

Tony stepped closer. "Now give me that book."

Jake stepped behind Caroline. Daria decided it was now or never. She tackled Tony. A second later, Jake tackled Caroline.

A shot fired. Tony dropped to the ground, yelling and holding his shoulder. Jake pulled Caroline's hands behind her back and secured her weapon.

Daria scooped up Tony's weapon, retrieved her pistol, then returned and pulled Tony to his feet. He bellowed in pain.

McDaniel, Cramer and Evans made it to the scene just as Daria and Jake subdued their threats. "Cuff them," Daria said.

Jake stepped in front of Caroline. "Where is my baby? What have you done with her?"

"Wouldn't you like to know?" She sneered. "You messed up my life. Now I'll mess up yours."

Daria motioned for Jake to join her. "Our weak link is over here," she said. "Tony isn't a true criminal. He'll crack."

Daria approached Tony, who was in obvious pain. "Where is the baby? You know Caroline will try to pin everything on you and make everyone believe you arranged the kidnapping, too. You're looking at life in prison if you don't tell us where to find Emma."

"I'm not supposed to tell." He rolled his head back and groaned.

"The sooner you talk, the faster you'll get to the hospital." Daria stepped back and eyed him. "Where is the baby?"

Jake stepped forward and lifted his fist.

Tony cowered under Jake's threat. "Okay, okay. The little girl is in a cabin out in the woods. I don't know the area, but it's close to a power line. Caroline's housekeeper is watching her and keeping a fire in the woodstove until we get back."

"You're Tony Schneider, aren't you?" Daria clenched her fists.

"How nice of you to remember me." He rolled his eyes. "You arrested my son a while back. We were none too happy for your intrusion on our father/son vacation. Mrs. Caroline saw what happened. She agreed that you were out of control and offered us a job. She paid good. I didn't know it involved a kid."

Jake pulled him up by the collar. "Which way from here?"

He nodded behind them. "About two miles into the forest."

Daria and Jake took off running to the truck. Robert stood there with the driver's door of his truck open, waiting for them with the engine running.

"How'd you get here?" Jake asked.

"McDaniel picked me up. Officers are watching my house while I'm gone." Robert got in the driver's seat.

"A cabin about two miles east." Daria opened the passenger door and hopped in.

"I could trek through the woods and get there faster." Jake balked at getting into the truck.

"We know the area, Jake. Get in. We can hike once we reach the top of the ridge." Daria motioned him into the vehicle.

He hesitated. "Emma must be okay if they have someone watching her." He let out a huff and slid in beside Daria. "At least we know she wasn't left out in the cold."

Robert turned the heat thermostat and fan on high. "I'll get you to the ridge in record time." He rolled away from the dairy farm.

Jake drummed his fingers on the dash. His body was still in search-and-rescue mode, but his insides were aching to hold his baby. How could he have gotten so attached to this little person so fast? He imagined her soft hands patting his cheek. He swallowed the emotion, trying to break him down.

"There are three cabins in the area Tony mentioned." Daria reached out and stopped him from drumming his fingers. She squeezed his hand. "We'll check them all unless we see one with smoke coming from the chimney."

Robert stopped in the middle of the icy road. "Here you go. I'll wait here for a text, then I'll drive on around to the gravel road and meet you there. Wouldn't want to alert anyone of our arrival by taking you closer."

"Got it." Jake hopped out of the truck and waited for Daria.

She tossed Robert the black book. "You should hold on to this for us." She turned back to Jake. "Let's do this."

Jake walked beside Daria until the forest thickened. He stepped ahead of her. She gripped his arm. "I'm still the law and I have jurisdiction."

"Don't go pulling rank on me right now." Jake stiffened his lip. "We're in this together, and we're rescuing Emma."

"I know, but we still have to use caution and do everything according to the law, or it might get thrown out of court." She pushed a snow-covered branch out of her face, knocking the snow on her coat.

Jake's big hand reached over her and held the branch back until he passed. "Unless there's no one left to take to court."

"Jake Fisher, I'm going to ignore that comment."

Jake focused ahead. "There in the middle of the valley. Look through the trees. Three cabins. Two have smoke drifting from the chimneys."

"I see. But which cabin?" Daria's breath fogged in the frosty air.

A flag went up in his gut. Was this a setup? Were there armed guards hiding out? He stopped and squatted. Daria did the same.

"What is it?" She eased her hand up and pulled at the branches of a snowy bush. The snow fell off and sprinkled to the ground. "Did you see something?"

He couldn't help but notice her big brown eyes searching the area. He trusted her and couldn't see himself raising Emma without her by his side.

"Something tells me we're walking into a trap." He pulled his weapon again. "I could be wrong, but my gut is usually on target."

"Okay." Daria retrieved her weapon. "How about we ease around to the back of the cabin on the left and check it first?"

"You've got it." Jake turned, still in a bent position, and crept through the forest as Daria suggested. He stopped and threw his hand up for her to stop.

"I saw that." Daria squatted lower. "Two armed men. They could be deer hunters."

"But look at the guns." Jake leaned close to her ear. "Those are not deer rifles."

"You're right," she whispered. "I could walk up and knock on the door while you stay hidden and cover me. Might be nothing. Maybe we're being too cautious."

"Did you just say that? Can a cop in an investigation ever be too cautious?" He eyed her.

"That's not what I meant. If they see us out here tiptoeing through the snow, making tracks everywhere, they will wonder what we're up to and could shoot without asking. We don't know if those men have anything to do with the case."

"You're right. Maybe I look for enemy activity too much." He dropped his shoulders, but his mind stayed on alert. He wasn't buying it at all.

"Let's go peek in the window. If there's no evidence of wrongdoing, I'll go to the front door."

"I'm not comfortable with you putting your life on the line like that." Jake put his hand on her back. "Maybe I should go."

"Jake, stop. Let's just move and see how it plays

out." She hunched over and ran to the side of the cabin by a window.

He followed suit and stopped on the opposite side of the same window, then eased up and peeked inside. Not two, but three armed men were inside. One man stood at the side of the front window, holding the curtain so he could look out. Another disappeared into a room carrying his weapon. The third man walked toward the window where Jake and Daria were.

Jake widened his eyes at her and pressed himself against the log cabin. Again, Daria did as he did. He prepared himself for battle.

"Hey, Joe, maybe Caroline did away with them." One man's voice carried through the cabin's wall.

The man turned away. His footsteps clomped across the floor. "That would save us from having to do the job."

Daria stared at him. Her nostrils flared and her lips tightened. She nodded toward the forest.

He eased up and checked the position of the men. Only the one at the front window remained in position. Could be a good thing or a bad thing. Before he could swing around, snow crunched behind him.

"Well, who do we have here, but the cop and the marine who have caused all the problems with our operation." The man's bushy eyebrows lowered and almost covered his deep-set, dark eyes. His rough, stocky exterior exuded killer experience.

Another man reached around Jake and Daria and took their weapons. "Making things easier on us, ay?"

"Not intentionally." Jake broke his silence and looked

at Daria. He motioned with his eyes for her to watch the other guy until the timing was right to fight back.

Daria gave him a slight nod. Smart girl. She understood.

Jake evaluated his next move. If he allowed the men to take him and Daria inside, they'd either be killed or beaten and left for dead. He couldn't let that happen. Now was their chance to overtake these two men and pray the third didn't show up and put a stop to it all.

"Inside." The two men walked behind Jake and Daria toward the front door.

Jake's eyes met Daria's. He nodded slightly and spun, ramming his shoulder into one man's diaphragm. Daria had knocked the other man down, and they were rolling on the ground, fighting.

"Hold your hands up or I'll shoot." The threat came from the third man who had been in the cabin.

The fighting stopped. Jake had to come up with another plan.

"No, you hold your hands up or *we* will shoot." A demand from a familiar voice came from the edge of the woods.

Jake straightened and turned around. He'd never been so relieved to see Robert standing there with his gun, plus McDaniel, Cramer, Evans and two other officers. They cuffed the men and put them in their squad cars.

"Boy, are we happy to see you guys." Daria patted her brother on the back. "Thank you for showing everyone where to find us. Your timing was perfect. Now we've got to find Emma."

Jake took his and Daria's weapons back from the men. He handed her pistol to her. "Emma must be in that other cabin with the smoke coming from the chimney. I'm not waiting any longer."

"I'm going with you." Daria caught up with him.

"You're not leaving me out on this one." Robert fell in beside them.

They traipsed together through the snow and uneven terrain to the other cabin with their weapons in a ready position in case of additional trouble. Before they reached the front door, a young woman opened the door, holding Emma wrapped in a thick fuzzy blanket.

Daria kept her weapon pointed at the lady. "Hand over the baby and back away with your hands up."

Jake ran and took Emma from her arms. Emma kicked her feet and squeezed him around the neck. This is the reunion he'd imagined. She loved him. His heart melted for his little niece.

"What's going on?" The young girl's eyes held fear. "Caroline hired me to babysit her niece. You can't take her."

"You've been misled." Daria handcuffed the girl. "This child was abducted and is now back with her family."

"I didn't know." The girl burst into tears. "I didn't know."

"The officers will take you to the police station and question you. If they determine you are innocent of the crime, they will let you go," Daria explained.

Jake cuddled Emma in his arms as he watched the young girl get in the back of a squad car.

Daria stepped up beside him. "It's tough watching someone young get arrested. Just remember, she's innocent until proven guilty."

"I know. I'm certain they used her." He looked down at Emma. She held a dirty, scarred sippy cup out to him. He cringed at the sight of it and took it from her. Instead of crying, she patted his face with both hands and kissed his nose. What a relief to see her unharmed and smiling. He'd hand over her clean cup when they got back to the truck.

Daria's hand gripped his forearm. "We need to get Emma out of here. Somewhere safe and warm."

FOURTEEN

After getting Emma back to Robert's house and enjoying everyone doting over her safe return, Daria received a call to come to the station. Disappointed at the interruption, she dismissed herself and headed toward the door.

She eased out of the house and hopped into Robert's truck. The passenger door opened just as she slid into the driver's seat. Jake sat smiling at her.

"Did you think you could just walk away and not be noticed?" Jake placed his hand on her arm. "You were spectacular today."

"Wasn't all me." Daria cut her eyes over at him. "We worked together as a team, and with the help of my colleagues, it appears we've solved your sister and brother-in-law's murder, arrested everyone involved with Emma's abduction and those involved with the bank's embezzlement scheme."

"Where are you headed now?" Jake buckled his seat belt. "Emma is in safe hands with your family."

"They want me to come down to the station. I suppose they want me in on the interrogation. This entire case has been so bizarre." Daria backed out of the driveway and drove down the road. "Do you really think we caught everyone? I keep getting this gnawing in my stomach that we're missing someone."

Jake's stare and pursed lips let her know he was pondering her comment. She could be wrong. Regardless, listening to the men explain their involvement might put all the pieces together and put her at rest.

"Are you thinking of a hired source or someone else at the top?" Jake turned and faced the street. "Could be a hidden source like in the war. Once you think you have everyone, there's that primary target slipping away unscathed. I'll have to trust your lead on this one. You are the law."

Daria laughed. "It's about time you admitted my status."

"I've known my limits all along. I just wanted to see you stand your ground. I love how tough and outspoken you've become over the years."

"Tough? I don't see myself like that." She turned on Main Street and headed to the station, yet again. "As much as I love my job, I'm not married to it. It has its upside and its downside, like any job does."

Traffic was calm. The slushy streets began melting with the sun's rays beaming down. Her thoughts drifted. She'd lived in Kimbleton long enough to know the weather could change in a matter of minutes. Christmas was only two days away. More snow would come, and she hadn't finished her shopping.

"Look, there are a lot of squad cars at the station. Is there some kind of special meeting going on?" Jake's comment brought her back to the present.

"I don't know." She pulled into the parking lot. "Let's go see."

Her stomach knotted. What could be so important that most of her coworkers gathered at one time, and no one told her? Was it another stab at her incompetence?

Jake opened the door for her. She stepped inside. McDaniel and Cramer greeted her. They ushered her to the conference room where other officers sat and stood around the walls. They had saved a seat for her at the table.

"What's going on, McDaniel?" Her pulse increased as she readied herself for more hazing and embarrassment. The serious look on Jake's face told her he was uncertain, too. He moved through the crowded room and stood over her. He rested a hand on her shoulder.

The room grew silent, which made perspiration form on her brow. Maybe she was going to be fired in front of everyone. She sat tall in the chair and waited.

McDaniel cleared his throat, and her eyes met his. "Your fellow officers and I realize what an outstanding and intuitive officer of the law you are, Daria. You've been steady and devout in your job and shown mercy in cases that shouldn't have received mercy. Then you stepped into the biggest, most corrupt case in our tourist town's history."

"That's true on all counts," Cramer interrupted.

McDaniel continued. "Because of your concerned comment earlier about how something still wasn't right, I took it on myself once I returned to the office to watch our security camera's recording of activity inside the office."

Daria cocked her head and looked up at him. "Security cameras inside the office?"

"Yes. Cramer and I suspected a rogue officer, so we installed hidden cameras." McDaniel looked around the room. "Sorry, everyone, we had to find the leak."

"We all know Lieutenant Jeffers played a big role in this entire ordeal, and at first, we thought we'd nailed the responsible party."

Daria sucked in a breath when Jeffers stepped into the room. Had he been released? Would her heart stop from shock? She must have really messed up.

Jeffers walked over and shook Daria's hand. "Things weren't as they seemed. That's why I permitted the security cameras. You and your marine friend helped draw out the rogue officer. After they took me into custody, and just before Jake spotted the flash drives in Cramer's office, the camera captured Evans sneaking around and tossing them inside. He threatened my family a few weeks ago and said if I told anyone about large sums of money randomly deposited into my account, my wife and kids would pay."

Daria couldn't believe what she was hearing. Evans, the rogue agent? No way.

Jeffers continued. "He had pictures of my kids getting on the school bus, my wife at the grocery store, my family and I enjoying time together at a restaurant. I was uncertain how to stop his harassment because he had people on the outside I was unaware of."

McDaniel chimed in. "We're all a team here, covering each other's backs. We want to thank Officer Daria Gordon and her marine friend, Jake Fisher, for their persistence in this case and for forcing Evans to expose his involvement on camera. Everyone's dismissed."

My marine? She liked the sounds of Jake being hers.

Daria's stomach churned. She didn't deserve the recognition, but thankfully her intuition was right. There had been one last person. Why did it have to be one of their own?

Several of the officers walked by and either shook her hand or gave her a fist bump or a high five. One officer stopped and handed her a bottle of shaving cream.

"Here, we don't need this anymore, Officer Gordon. Fine job."

By the time they'd all left the room, Daria sat and stared at the wall. It was over. Finally, over. A calm washed over her. She'd been fully accepted by her team. What a satisfying feeling.

Jeffers stuck his head back into the conference room. "Daria, get a car off the back lot and take that few days off I suggested. Get some rest. Enjoy your Christmas."

"Yes, sir. Thank you." Daria stood and faced Jake. "Let's go back to Robert and Gina's where we can share the good news with them and celebrate over a big cup of hot chocolate with lots of miniature marshmallows."

"How about we stop and have a few uninterrupted moments at the diner before joining your family?" Jake took her hand. "I'd like to have some quiet time with just you."

Daria's cheeks warmed. Had she blushed? Maybe he didn't notice.

"Sounds nice. I'd love to." She exited the police station. "Do you want to drive Robert's truck? I'll meet you there in one of the unmarked cars."

"Sure thing." Jake hopped into the truck and drove away.

Daria sat in her new police car for a moment and

took in some deep breaths. Saddened by Evans's deceit. Thrilled over Jeffers's return. Glad the case was over. Now she needed to talk to Jake, and meeting at the restaurant would be the perfect time.

December in the mountains was always a beautiful sight, even though clouds had rolled in and blocked the afternoon sun. The added layer of snow made it really look like Christmas. She pulled out onto the busy street with a whole new outlook on her life. God had made a way for her far above what she'd ever imagined.

Jake parked in the restaurant's empty parking lot and waited for Daria. His life lay before him, raising his sister's beautiful daughter, and that was a heartwarming fact. Although he'd like to add Daria to his life permanently, he didn't want to push her. They'd both just come through an emotional and dangerous ordeal. Maybe tonight wasn't the night to talk.

He spotted her turning into the parking lot. She pulled in beside him. He hopped out and met her at her car door. Something he enjoyed doing. She stood and their eyes met. He couldn't help himself. He put his hands on both sides of her face and gave her a quick kiss.

"Just to congratulate you on a job well done." He took her hand as they walked inside together.

"Thanks, but you should be congratulated, too." She squeezed his hand.

There was a definite connection between them. He escorted her to the booth by the window, noting no one else was there except for one server. Maybe the kitchen crew, but he couldn't see them. Where was everyone? Too early for the dinner crowd? Christmas music played in the background. He hadn't been big into the holidays for the past several years. Amanda was the festive one. Well, his mom had been, too, when she was strong enough to move about freely.

He picked up the menu. "Do we want dinner or a snack with coffee or hot chocolate?"

"Hmm, I think dinner would be nice." She pushed the hair from her face.

They placed their orders. Daria asked for hot chocolate and made it sound so tasty. He ordered one, too. It wouldn't be like Gina's, filled with miniature marshmallows, but he'd go for it, anyway.

Daria folded her hands and placed them on the table in front of her. "Such a great idea to come here. I can finally relax and breathe."

"Speaking of relaxing." He smiled. "I thought this would be a good time to have a serious conversation." He reached over and put his hand on top of her folded hands. "Are you up for it after all we've been through?"

Her eyes fell on his hand, covering hers. "I think so. What do you want to talk about?"

"Us." Jake swallowed hard. "Me returning to Kimbleton and meeting up with my best friend from middle school cannot be an accident. We were always together having fun."

Daria moved her hand on top of his.

His heart thumped hard against his chest. "I know having Emma in my life now puts a unique twist in a budding relationship."

"Jake." Daria's eyes sparkled with the blinking lights around the window.

"Daria, I need you to hear me out."

The server delivered their hot chocolates.

He continued. "I know I've only been back in town a few days, but I feel like it's been longer." Frustration crawled over him. Why couldn't he just say it? He loved her and wanted her in his life forever.

Just tell her.

A woman slowly entered the restaurant all bundled up with only her weary-looking eyes peering above the thick multi-colored scarf covering her face, and a floppy, wide brimmed hat that barely exposed her brown hair. Her movements appeared wobbly. She glanced around before turning toward them and approaching their table. Cautiously, she slid into the booth beside Daria and put a small handgun to Daria's head. "She's coming with me."

"No. She's not." Jake stiffened. He wasn't about to make any quick moves. The lady might pull the trigger.

"Yes, she is. And don't try to stop me." Her eyes narrowed.

With the table dividing them, Jake evaluated his next move. This person was the enemy right now. He curled his fingers into a fist. His knuckles whitened.

"Don't think for one minute I don't know what you're planning." She grabbed Daria's arm. "Come with me if you want to live."

Jake's eyes met Daria's.

You know I'll come for you, right?

Daria had to know he wouldn't let her leave the property with this woman. He'd settle these threats once and for all. The pulsating rushing through his body screamed attack, but he must wait for the right moment.

"It's okay, Jake," Daria said as she eased from the booth.

Her controlled tone relaxed him, knowing she had her head together. She was a trained police officer and could handle the situation. Right? He wouldn't let her out of his sight.

"Yes, as long as no one gets in my way, she might make it." The woman stood tall and determined, still pressing the pistol to Daria's temple. "So, don't get in my way, Jake."

She backed out of the restaurant with Daria and shifted the weapon to Daria's side. Jake jumped to his feet and stood by the booth, waiting for the right moment to make his move.

I need Your wisdom, God.

Patrons began filling the parking lot and trailing inside. Why now when he was trying to keep his eyes on Daria? Once the woman moved out of sight from the window, Jake darted out of the restaurant's back door and around to the side of the building. There were too many tourists and children trailing into the area. He couldn't counterattack. It was too risky.

The woman made Daria get in an old station wagon. Not a smart getaway vehicle. While the woman walked around to the driver's side, Daria dropped something out of the window. Why didn't she try to run when the woman walked away from her door? Guess she had her reasons. The car pulled toward the exit, but traffic blocked their immediate escape. Jake eased around the parking lot. What had Daria dropped on the ground? He searched until he spotted her car keys almost buried in the snow.

Smart move.

He hopped into her vehicle and fell in line with the parking lot traffic. The station wagon pulled in front of another car and onto the street. Jake kept a keen eye on the vehicle. He couldn't lose them. Who was this woman? They thought they'd solved the case.

Jake chewed his lip while some people weren't focusing on driving. Their fingers danced across the tiny keyboard of their cells. Irritation arose. His lack of patience in a desperate situation teetered on anger.

Breathe. Stay calm. Think.

The car was getting away, and he couldn't lose sight of it. He pulled out of the parking lot's traffic line and found an opening at the corner of the asphalt. The car bounced as he drove off the curb. A horn honked behind him, and the man shook all kinds of hand gestures at him. But he'd made it onto the street, and no one had gotten hurt. Only two cars behind Daria.

That's what I'm talking about. Smart maneuver if I do say so.

The car in front of him turned onto another road, leaving one car between him and Daria. Where was the woman taking her? Did she plan on harming Daria? Jake slid down in the driver's seat just enough to drive safely and in hopes of not being identified by the abductor.

Their vehicle eased across the slushy road and made a slow turn into a neighborhood. The woman wasn't much of a getaway driver. She eased down the street and made another turn into a cove. Jake made slow turns and pulled to the curb close to the cove.

He stepped out of the car and walked up the sidewalk. The woman pulled into a garage and closed the door. He crossed the street and sneaked up to the house. Car doors slammed. Then another door slammed. Why a neighborhood home? He eased around to the back of the house and peeked inside the living room window. The light-colored sheers kept him from seeing clearly, but at least he had a view and could catch most of what they said.

Daria sat on the sofa while the lady tossed off her hat, scarf and long coat. She sat in a chair across from Daria, still holding the gun. Her grip on the weapon wasn't proper, nor was her finger on the trigger. No apparent threat there, but one couldn't be too relaxed in any armed situation.

The faint laughter of kids met his ears. The lady slid her weapon between the cushion and armrest before two small children ran into the room and jumped into the woman's lap. They laughed and hugged her. Their mom? The whole abduction didn't make sense. She wrapped her arms around the kids while Daria watched.

A man entered the room from what looked like a hallway and crossed over toward the woman. His wife? His family? Jake stiffened. He looked familiar. When the man turned and faced the woman, Jake blinked and stared inside as best he could. How had Officer Evans made it home when he was supposed to be in jail?

FIFTEEN

Daria studied the scene before her. Evans? Why put his wife at risk of getting hurt when she could have simply asked her to come over? After all, they'd met a few times even though they hadn't talked in a while. She looked pale.

"Evans, what's going on?" Did he have a weapon? She didn't feel threatened. "How'd you get out of jail?"

"My wife borrowed money from the equity of our house and bailed me out." He stared at her, then shoved his hands in his pockets. "It was a really dumb thing for me to have my wife kidnap you in her condition, and I'm the blame for it. She could have gotten hurt." Evans rubbed his wife's shoulder with one hand. "The department thinks I went rogue, but you should know things aren't the way they seem."

"I've heard that before, but I'm listening." Daria maintained her composure when she spotted Jake through the sheers. He'd found the car keys and followed them like a good cop or marine would.

"You remember I told you Karla hasn't been feeling well?" He paced. "I didn't explain her condition. I just brushed it off as a stomach bug or something."

"I remember, but what does that have to do with anything?"

"The doctor diagnosed her with lymphoma a few months ago. She's been losing weight and tired all the time. Fever, itching and coughing." His daughter ran and grabbed his legs. He picked her up. "Gregory Hall sent a message for me to meet him at the coffee shop. He'd heard about Karla."

Daria scooted to the edge of the sofa. "Did you meet with him? What did he want?"

Evans let the child down and sat in a chair closer to Daria. "He said he'd looked at my bank account and knew I didn't have the funds for chemo treatments and he'd like to make a donation. I was stunned. Did he have a right to look at my account?" He rubbed his forehead. "I accepted a large 'donation' from him. A really large donation. Something about it didn't sit well with me."

Blackmail? Money laundering? Daria figured it out before he completed his story. She couldn't believe Evans was involved in the case, but the evidence in that security video was hard to ignore. Gregory Hall used him, then threatened him and his family.

Where did Jake go?

She squinted at the window. Jake wasn't there. Evans looked toward the window and jumped up.

"What is it? Someone there?" He ran over and scrambled for the pistol his wife held earlier.

"Just me." Jake stepped into the room from the kitchen.

Evans spun and pointed the pistol at him. "How'd you find us?"

"Evans, stop," Daria said. "Jake is on our side. This

entire investigation started with his sister, who was killed, along with his brother-in-law."

Daria filled Jake in on what Evans had already shared. She turned back to Evans, who had put his gun on top of the bookcase away from the kids' reach.

"Go ahead and finish your story." She needed to hear him say what had happened.

"When Gregory realized his files went missing, his wife became furious. Caroline, I believe. I'm not sure which one of them was more involved because she was in his office almost more than he was. She may have started the whole donation thing to pull me in since I'm a cop and use me for their schemes.

"Those toy flash drives were an ingenious idea by your sister, Jake. She was a smart and brave lady, and I'm sorry for your loss. Anyway, Gregory suddenly demanded his 'donation' back." He made air quotations with his fingers. "I gave him back as much as I could, but it wasn't enough to satisfy him. I'd used part of it for medical bills. That's when he said if he got caught, he'd point a finger at me and make it look like I went rogue. As you can tell, he succeeded. I'm a cop and I don't know how to clear myself."

Jake slammed his fist into his other palm. "That's the way it goes with traitors. Daria and I will figure it out."

"Evans, I need you to come down to the station to give your statement." Daria stood. "I'm not going to press charges, but I need this information documented."

"I can't do that. You can record my statement here, but I'm not showing my face until I'm cleared. I appreciate you not arresting me or pressing charges."

"You're her friend." Jake walked over and stood by her side.

She glanced at him, then looked at Evans and his wife. "We've been in the department together for years and friends for a long time. Jake and I will handle things from here. You stay put. We'll be back to get your statement."

"One more thing. I owe Cramer and the department a huge apology. After Gregory started threatening me, I bought some of those rubber flash drives and tossed them in Cramer's office trying to save myself. Those drives are empty. You can check them." Evans walked them to the door. "I'm sorry for the trouble I've caused everyone. I really didn't mean any harm, but you've always been a reasonable cop. I knew you'd listen before judging me."

Daria walked outside, joined by Jake. "How could one case get so entangled in greed?"

"The world is filled with all types of people with different values in life. Some are good and, well, some aren't." Jake pointed toward the street. "I'm parked just around the corner."

"Let's run by the station and go back for his statement." Chills rushed over her body after being inside Evans's warm house. "I'd like to get this case straightened out before Christmas."

"Me, too," Jake said. "We've got a lot to talk about."

Daria paused and studied him. "I suppose we do."

Hope it's about our future. Together, that is.

By the time they reached the car, her fingers were almost frozen. Jake tossed her the keys. She barely caught them. A warm car, a cozy house and a good night's rest sounded delightful, but first things first. She couldn't leave Evans hanging. His interview was top priority.

As the day ended—after the trip from Evans's home to the station, back to Evans's, then finally to her brother's house for a hot dinner and restful evening—Daria's thoughts swirled with questions.

How should she approach Jeffers about Evans? Would he be open to hearing Evans's side of the story? Would his friends, especially Cramer, at the department welcome him back or would they see him as untrustworthy? Would they put him on probation or charge him? Could they possibly find compassion for Evans and his family?

She and Jake pulled into her brother's driveway. A leaning snowman, disturbed clots of snow and small footprints in the front yard showed the kids had had a blast in the wintry weather.

Gina opened the front door, holding Emma.

Daria and Jake got out of the car.

"I saw you drive up," Gina said. "Dinner's ready."

"You are amazing." Daria hugged Gina and kissed Emma on the way inside. "And I'm starving."

"I'm ready for some grub. Smells good." Jake scooped his baby from Gina's arms and went straight to the kitchen.

Isaac and Alexa ran and hugged her around the waist. One day, she prayed she'd have a family of her own to run into her arms.

"We're waiting." Robert's voice trailed into the living room, drawing Daria back from her dreams.

She joined everyone around the kitchen table and breathed in the spicy aroma. Homemade chili with shredded cheese was a perfect meal for a frosty, snowy night. Isaac and Alexa rattled on and on about how much fun they'd had building a snowman, then running and tackling him. Emma slapped her little hands on the table.

"Here. Let me put her in the high chair," Gina said as she took her from Jake.

Daria closed her eyes at the first bite and savored the flavor. "So delicious. I needed this. Thank you, Gina, for all your hospitality. No wonder I love you so much. My brother could never cook. Good thing he's got you."

"Aw, it's the least I can do to help all of you during this dangerous situation," Gina said.

Daria finished her meal, then rinsed hers and Jake's bowls and placed them in the dishwasher. "Robert, when you have time, we need to speak with you about our latest findings."

"I have something to discuss with you, as well." Robert placed a toothpick in his mouth, pushed back from the table and crossed his legs.

Her curiosity piqued. What information would Robert have after staying home all day? He should have enjoyed his snow day off work and spending time with family.

"I'll finish cleaning up the dishes." Gina cleaned off the table and wiped down the counter. "Okay, kiddos. Go to your rooms and play." She gave Robert a kiss, then wiped Emma's hands and face before taking her out of the high chair and leaving the kitchen. "I'll be in the living room."

Daria leaned forward and placed her elbows on the table. "We need to talk about Evans."

"Just the person I need to talk to you about." Robert

uncrossed his legs and leaned toward her. "Word on the street is he was framed, just like Jeffers. Only Jeffers discovered the money and confronted Gregory Hall. That's when Jeffers started receiving threats on his family's life if he exposed the embezzlement operation."

"Whoa. Do you believe the rumor?" Jake asked.

"I received an email from four police officers who were on a different shift from you, Daria. They requested an online meeting with me since I'm in investigations. So, I set it up. We met early this afternoon. They didn't believe Evans went rogue even though that video incriminates him as he tried to place blame on Cramer. Both are exemplary officers. Jeffers, too."

Jake drummed his fingers on the table. Daria reached over, placed her hand on top of his and stopped the noise.

"Evans is out on bail. His wife borrowed against their equity to get him out," Daria said. "And I have a recorded statement from him about what happened. It implicates Gregory Hall, and his wife, Caroline. And get this—they had hired Richard, that kid I arrested, and his dad, Tony, to help get rid of Jake and me."

"I'm proud of you, being so efficient. My baby sister, the cop, pulling the case of a century in Kimbleton to a close." Robert's smile showed his approval.

"She is amazing, isn't she?" Jake took her hand.

Her cheeks warmed as Jake and Robert smiled at her. She'd proven herself as a dedicated, successful police officer, and the two men she loved approved of her actions. What more could she ask?

Robert stood and stretched. "If Evans's story matches the online meeting information I received today, his bail money will be refunded. Then outside of court hearings and sentencing of all the guilty parties, the case will be closed."

Daria played Evans's statement as they drank coffee and munched on peach cobbler à la mode. Robert nodded and made notes and Jake sat quietly as if he were devouring every detail even though he'd already heard it.

"Evans is now worried we will charge his wife for kidnapping." Daria took the last bite of her cobbler. "I'm not pressing charges. In fact, we need to take up a donation for her treatments. What do you think, Robert?"

"No harm was done. And Evans's statement is consistent with the CI's and with those of the officers I met with. The charges against him will be dropped, although he may get probation over trying to implicate Cramer."

Daria leaned her head back and closed her eyes.

Thank You, God, for answering my prayer and bringing out the truth.

Jake stretched his arms back and popped his neck. "Where is my little munchkin? I need some more Emma snuggles." He went into the living room where Gina sat reading a children's book to her. She looked up, slid from Gina's lap and ran to him.

He picked her up and tossed her in the air.

She giggled. "Again."

He did it again, then kissed her on the neck. Hearing her laugh made his mood even lighter. Emma straightened her legs and leaned toward the floor.

"I know, little lady, you want down." Jake softened his deep voice. "I'm learning what you like and don't like."

A weight had lifted from his shoulders. His sister and

brother-in-law's murderer was behind bars. He could now grieve their loss and enjoy the part of them left behind. Emma.

Daria stood by the fireplace, laughing as Emma laughed. Such a pleasant sound. The two ladies he loved enjoying themselves. Would Daria consider a closer relationship? She'd said she loved him. They still needed to talk.

Daria's cell rang. He focused on her as she talked. A sparkle appeared in her eyes. What? Something good for a change? He surveyed the room and noted each person's location. Something he'd done daily in Afghanistan. One never knew when he'd have to protect them.

"Jake." Daria tapped on his arm. "Did you hear me?"

Of course he did, but he was in protective mode. "Yep, I heard you."

Her hands plopped on her waist. "What did I say?" Her smirky smile meant she didn't believe him.

"You said the windows have been replaced, and the walls repaired. My house is ready for us to return home." He winked. "See, I can multitask, too. Guess I could get packed up."

"It's late. The slush on the streets has frozen over again." Daria stepped in front of him. "You may as well stay another night here and enjoy some relaxation for a change."

Jake had the urge to pull her into his arms, but with Gina and Robert in the room, he figured it wouldn't be appropriate.

"Sounds good. Tomorrow it is." Jake slid his arms into his coat and picked up Emma's coat. "Come on, Amanda junior. Let's go to our apartment."

Gina rose from the sofa and moved toward him. "Why don't you leave her here and get yourself a good night's sleep before you leave tomorrow?"

"I want to spend time with her regardless of whether she sleeps or not." Jake picked her up. "I've been away from her long enough. We need more bonding time."

Daria took Emma's coat and put it on her, pulling the hood up over her head. "I'll walk you two over there."

Jake stepped outside in the frigid weather. He ducked Emma's head and pressed it against his chest until he reached the top of the apartment stairs. Daria stood on the step behind him. He unlocked the door and stepped into the warmth with Daria on his heels.

Emma straightened her legs and wanted down. She ran from room to room while Daria and Jake sat on the sofa. Emma brought back a pink pillow and tossed it on the floor, then tried to sit on it. She slid off and placed her head on it, rubbing her eyes.

"Looks like someone is ready for bed." Daria got up and retrieved a pair of warm pajamas for Emma. "Do you want to change her, or would you like for me to do it?"

"Uh, I'll let you." He would practice the changing of clothes when no one was around. It wasn't the same as dismantling a weapon and putting it back together. The gun didn't wiggle around as his niece did.

While Daria tended to Emma, Jake turned on the gas fireplace and went to the kitchen to make hot chocolate. He went back to the living room and placed two cups of hot chocolate on the small coffee table. In a matter of minutes, Daria had Emma changed, her bottle fixed and placed her in her bed. He lifted his eyebrows. She was a lady of many talents.

"That was fast. I know who to call when I need help with Emma." His heart rate picked up speed. Now would be the perfect time to have that serious talk.

"You know I'll help anytime you need. Oh, you made us some hot chocolate. Nice." She sat back on the sofa, holding her drink with both hands. "Thank you for all of your help with this case. In fact, if it weren't for you, we may have never known about the criminal activity taking place right here in Kimbleton."

"It all worked out. I inherited a baby, met up with you again, and I succumbed to your authority." He held his cup up. "A toast. Miracles never cease in this marine's life. Semper fi."

She laughed and bumped her cup to his. "That means always faithful, right?" She placed her cup on the table.

"You've got it." He put his cup down beside hers. Bravery was his specialty, but confronting the love of his life about his feelings for her almost had him cowering.

Why am I so nervous? God, help me remain calm.

Jake took in a deep breath and slowly released it. He turned his focus completely on her. Their eyes met. He reached over and took her hand in his. "Daria, you know I love you. I never dreamed my life could be so complete this soon after returning from overseas."

Silence.

She stared at him and didn't say anything. He searched her beautiful face, waiting for a response.

She placed her other hand on top of his. "Jake, I lost you once, and I don't plan on losing you again. I've already told you that I love you, too."

He wrapped his arms around her and pulled her close. *Thank You, God.*

Her arms wrapped around him about the time his lips pressed against hers. Smooth and warm. The moment he pulled back and looked at her, she placed her hand on his chest.

"I'd better go. We both need our rest after all we've been through. I'll help you and Emma get settled in the house tomorrow. Then we can talk some more."

"Emma and I will be over in the morning for breakfast with everyone before we leave. I'll see you then." He kissed her again. "I love you."

"And I love you." She stepped out onto the porch. "See you in the morning."

Jake watched as she walked down the outdoor steps and into the side door of her brother's house. He went back inside and fell across his bed, thinking. Who knew two strong-willed childhood friends could see eye to eye as adults and fall in love? A trained marine and a skilled police officer raising his sister's baby together.

His body sank deeper into the mattress and his eyes grew heavy. Silence ruled the night. He rolled over still fully dressed.

God, You have done the unimaginable. Thank You for protecting us.

Morning arrived much too soon. Emma sat in her porta crib, jabbering and playing with her giraffe. Jake stepped inside her room and picked her up.

"Whoa. We need a hazmat team in here. Where's Daria when I need her?" He held Emma up under her arms and away from his body to keep from being contaminated, searching for a safe place to lay her down.

"Back to your crib, you go. I've got to prepare my-self for this task." He left the room, curling his nose. "I can do this."

He gathered the supplies necessary to change Emma's diaper, along with a trash bag, and tackled the un-fortunate problem. The clean diaper hung on crooked, but it stayed put.

"Oorah. We did it, Emma." He picked her up and gave her a light squeeze. "Love you, sweet girl. Let's go find Daria and have breakfast. Then we can go home."

"Bite." Emma reached her arm out, opening and clos-ing her hand.

"Exactly where we're going."

He pulled his coat on and put Emma's on her. A blis-tery wind blew, rustling the trees beside the house. Gray clouds covered the sky.

More snow coming. Guess we'll have a white Christ-mas.

Daria opened the side door to the house. "Good morn-ing. Come on in where it's warm."

Jake didn't waste any time getting Emma inside. She kicked her legs and stiffened. She wanted down. He took her over and Daria helped set her in the high chair.

The aroma of bacon frying made his mouth water. He glanced across the table at Daria and smiled. He never dreamed he'd have an instant family.

"After we get you and Emma packed up, I'll help you move back into your home, if you'd like." Daria continued eating.

"Sure," Jake said. "I'd like that. It'll be nice to be back in my own place. Robert, I appreciate the hospital-ity you and Gina have given Emma and me. I owe you."

"We're glad things got settled before Christmas." Gina poured Jake another cup of coffee. "Tomorrow is Christmas Eve. Maybe you'll have time to put up some decorations."

Decorate? Not sure where to start. Maybe next year after I'm settled.

"We'll see. My mom always took charge of decorations while I helped eat all the desserts." He pushed from the table. "Thank you, again, for everything. I'll run and get my things."

Within the hour, Jake stood at Daria's car, waiting for her to pop the trunk. She emerged from the front door with Emma, the diaper bag and another bag. He heard her cell beep, but she had her hands full and didn't check it. They loaded up and Daria drove them home.

Jake started a fire in the wood fireplace. He drew in a deep breath. Memories of growing up in his parents' home flashed through his mind. A pleasant, comforting thought. He glanced at Daria. Her love for Emma showed in her caring actions.

Daria's cell rang the same time as someone knocked on the front door. Jake exchanged glances with Daria and shrugged his shoulders. She answered her phone as he walked over and opened the door.

A man stuck a shotgun to his abdomen.

"We have unfinished business."

SIXTEEN

Daria's adrenaline skyrocketed as McDaniel warned her of Tony Schneider's escape and his threat against her. "He's here now," she whispered.

"Put that phone down," Tony yelled.

Daria sat on the sofa, holding Emma. She placed her phone on the coffee table. His hostile behavior and angry tone put her on high alert. She pulled Emma close to shield her should shooting start.

"What do you mean, we have unfinished business?" Jake's feet shuffled on the tile floor.

"Not you, her."

"You're supposed to be in jail." Daria pushed to her feet. She eased over to the porta crib and set Emma down. "What do you want with me, Tony?"

"Yeah, and what else is new?" Tony squared his shoulders. "I finagled my way out of those handcuffs and used them to break the back window out of the squad car. I ran into the woods before they knew I was gone. Figured you'd be here. Same place I found you before."

"You were one of the shooters who blew the windows out in Jake's house and risked the life of a baby. How could you have lived with yourself if the child died?"

"Enough talk. I need to settle a score, and if you make any sudden moves, I'll blow a hole in your friend's belly."

Daria exchanged glances with Jake. He didn't appear to be nervous. She looked at Emma before moving farther away from her crib. In case of an attack, Emma should be in the clear.

What are you thinking, Jake?

Tony poked Jake in the belly with his shotgun. "Back up."

Jake backed up. Daria stayed put. Tony closed the front door.

"Who hired you to find me?" Daria took a step forward.

"Stay put." He shuffled the weapon from Jake to her, then back to Jake. "Caroline left me a bag of money so I can escape to Mexico. All I have to do is make you pay for destroying her life and business. Besides, Richard is still suffering from humiliation after you arrested him. Teaming up with Gregory and Caroline is the most profitable business deal I've ever made."

"You don't really think I'm going to let you shoot her, do you?" Jake towered over Tony like a streetlamp over a park bench. His tone was steady and smooth.

"I'll shoot you first, then her, if you want to throw threats." Tony spat on the floor.

Daria fumed at his arrogance. Jake spun, and his foot came around and smacked him on the side of the head. Tony dropped to the floor, along with his gun.

"Did you knock him out?" Daria rushed over and felt for a pulse.

"Guess I did. I didn't kick him that hard." Jake huffed.

"His pulse is stable, but he's going to have your boot print on his face."

Another knock at the front door had her pulling her weapon. Jake opened the door. Evans, Cramer and Mc-Daniel stood there with their weapons drawn. A freshly cut spruce tree had been tossed on the lawn.

"Whoa. Don't shoot. It's just us," Cramer said. He pointed to Tony lying on the floor. "Looks like you've taken care of him."

Evans stepped forward, pulling out his handcuffs. "We were already on our way over here when we got the alert of Tony's escape. Did you get the message?"

Daria retrieved her cell and glanced at it before dropping it into her pocket. "I heard the phone's alert tone that I had a message, but we were loading the car and our hands were full. So, no, I didn't get to read the update. I'm glad you called."

Daria explained how the incident went down. Mc-Daniel assisted Evans, handcuffing their intruder.

"We will take care of him. You guys grab the tree we brought and try to enjoy the rest of your Christmas holiday." McDaniel walked out, helping Evans get Tony into the car.

Cramer paused. "You're safe now." He walked out and closed the door behind him.

"What just happened?" Jake threw his arm up. "Is this case over or not?"

"It's over. What I'm shocked about is seeing Evans and Cramer together. Jeffers must be working overtime to smooth things out and put the department back together."

Emma let out a squeal. She reached over the top of her crib and threw her giraffe on the floor.

"I think she wants out so she can run around." Daria

reached up and hugged Jake. He put his arm around her. A sense of security and warmth rushed over her. She backed away. "You just saved my life. I wasn't sure how I would take him down, but I would have taken a bullet for you and Emma."

"You would have figured something out. Besides, I'm the marine in the house. You should never have to take a bullet for me. Let me go get our tree." He kissed her on the cheek and went outside. A moment later, he dragged the spruce inside. "Let's get this tree up."

Daria picked Emma up and followed Jake to the garage. He'd left the tree laying on the living room floor.

"I see three boxes up on that shelf marked Christmas." Daria held Emma close and wrapped her arms snug around her. "It's too cold out here. I'm taking Emma inside."

In a matter of minutes, Jake walked into the kitchen carrying all three boxes. He pushed the door closed with his foot. Daria reminisced about the fun they'd had in their early years. Could her future with him be even better?

He took the boxes into the living room. "There has to be a tree stand in here somewhere." He opened one box. "Here it is. I don't know much about decorating a tree or raising a baby, but with your help, I guess I'll figure it out."

She put Emma on the floor and opened the other boxes while Jake added more wood to the fireplace. She pulled her phone out of her pocket and located some Christmas music. Emma shuffled around as she tried to dance.

They got the tree up and put lights on it. Using an artificial tree in the mountains didn't seem right. Enjoying family time and finding an actual tree always helped set the mood for the season. She hoped next year they could go out and find a real tree together with Emma.

"Now for the decorations." Jake reached in and started hanging silver balls on the tree. He lifted Emma and let her drop a small plastic icicle near the top. She stared at the lights and giggled.

Daria hung a few ornaments, bumping elbows with Jake occasionally. The setting was right for a perfect evening. She pulled out something wrapped in tissue paper.

"What's this?" She used caution unwrapping it. If Amanda thought it was that special, then she would be extra careful handling it.

Jake picked Emma up and stepped by Daria's side as a small picture in a Christmas frame fell into her hand. His eyes widened.

"I remember that day. We had fun decorating the tree while Mom took our pictures, but I did not know Amanda made a Christmas ornament out of it." Jake shook his head. "There's Amanda, you and me standing in front of the tree. And look, there in the background is my dad."

"What a treasure. Who would have known we'd be here right now, years later, and find this photo?" Daria slipped her arm around Jake's waist.

God, You orchestrated this reunion, didn't You?

Jake looked down at her and pulled her close. "Tell me. What did you mean when you said you weren't married to your job? What is your dream?"

Daria kissed Emma's little hand, then looked up at

him. "You are, Jake. You and Emma are my dreams come true."

He leaned over and brushed his lips against hers. Emma pushed at his face and laughed. He placed her on the floor in front of the twinkling Christmas lights, then faced Daria.

Daria's heart fluttered.

He lifted her chin with his finger and kissed her. She pulled back and looked into his eyes. Her life was complete. She'd renewed her faith, redeemed herself with the department and discovered that the missing piece from her life was Jake.

God knew the plans He had for her. What more could she ask for?

EPILOGUE

"Can you believe how much she's grown in the past eight months?" Jake picked Emma up and put her on his shoulders. He walked the paved trail toward the children's play area at the Mountain Top Park. "Life took a 180 after Amanda and Tom died. Emma has challenged me and made me learn to think of others above myself. I love her as my own. Reconnecting with you was a blessing I hadn't expected."

"Isn't it amazing how life takes a shift when we least expect it?" Daria handed Emma her cup. "Who knew I'd fall for an armed marine in the Marketplace parking lot who stirred up a hornet's nest of crime? You sure turned my world around."

The playground came into view. Colorful animals mounted on large springs, a bright red mini slide and a swing set with baby seats in different shades of blue.

Emma kicked her legs and shook her arms. Juice spilled from her cup and landed on Jake's head.

"Hey." He took her off his shoulders and put her down. "That wasn't a dripless cup, was it?" He brushed at his wet hair.

Daria bent over, laughing. "No. That was the new one you bought her."

"It's not funny." Jake chuckled. "Remind me to toss it when we get back to the house."

Emma took off running toward the park.

"Emma, wait." Jake picked up his pace with Daria trailing behind him. "Wait for Uncle Jake."

She stopped and pointed to the horse on a spring. "De, ride horsey."

"Yes, you can ride it." Daria caught up with her, took her hand and helped her up on the brown-and-white horse with a painted-on green saddle.

Jake found peace knowing Emma loved Daria and vice versa. "De" had become Daria's nickname since Emma couldn't say her name. He found himself calling her "De." He joined in and helped his little sweetheart ride all the animals, slide down the slide and swing until she became fussy.

"Is it nap time already?" Jake picked her up. She placed her head on his shoulder and patted his back. A tender feeling he'd never forget.

"There's a picnic table over there under the tree. I'll go get the basket and the blanket so she can take a nap." Daria left and came back with their lunch.

Jake had hoped Emma would go to sleep while they were at the park. He wanted some uninterrupted time with Daria.

"What did you pack in here?" Daria placed a table-cloth over the concrete picnic table and got the sand-wiches and canned drinks out of the basket.

"I packed what Emma likes. What else, but peanut

butter and jelly?" Jake laughed as he put Emma on the concrete bench. "She's almost too small to sit there."

Emma slapped her hands on the table. After a few bites, her eyes rolled and her jelly-covered hand rubbed her hair. Jake picked her up and moved her to the blanket they'd spread out on the ground.

Now I can talk to Daria. Why am I so nervous?

They cleaned up their trash and tossed it in the park's trash can. Jake sat beside Daria on the bench and took her hand.

"I love the mountains and the open air," Daria spoke softly. "Do you remember when your family and mine used to come here on Sunday afternoons after church? I don't think I admired the view then as I do now. So serene."

"I know. That's why I wanted us to come here." Jake swallowed the nervous lump in his throat and turned to face her. "Daria, we've talked about the future many times in the past few months. Emma loves you and I love you. I think it's time to make *us*, our relationship, permanent." He reached into his pants pocket and pulled out a small box. "Will you marry me?"

"Yes, yes, I will." Her eyes sparkled.

He put the diamond on her finger and kissed her. "Because of you and Emma, I am a better man."

"And because of God's perfect plan for us, we are a perfect family." Daria placed her hand gently on his cheek. "I love you, Jake Fisher."

"And I love you." Jake blew out the breath he'd held. "I'm glad that's settled. Now I have something else to tell you."

"Guess I'm going to have to teach you how not to

destroy a romantic moment." She laughed. "What's so important?"

"I heard from Jeffers yesterday. I'll start working investigations at the police department with Robert next week."

"That's wonderful. I want to be a stay-at-home, full-time mother figure for Emma. After we're married, I'll turn in my notice."

"Sounds like a plan to me." Jake put his arms around Daria and kissed her again. Emma sat up and rubbed her eyes. "Our girl is awake."

* * * * *